STORM CLOUD RISING
Book 1 of The Rain Trilogy

J. Richard Jacobs

STORM CLOUD RISING
Book 1 of The Rain Trilogy

DOUBLE DRAGON

Foreword

Science fiction writers. What an odd breed we are. Our speculations often take us to distant, fanciful places and times. We flippantly play the "What If" game with all sorts of exotic ideas and themes. We tinker with time. We go into galaxies unknown. Science frequently is stretched to the breaking point...sometimes beyond. We take trips to unknown worlds and visit alien species. We even make war with them, make love to them (no matter how unlikely that may be), and we come away...changed for the experience.

But there are changes that happen closer to home. Changes brought about by reasons that some would say are mundane. Profound changes.

Changes that will affect all of humanity for all time. Changes permanent in their nature. No aliens need apply. No wars are necessary. No cross breeding required.

The Rain Trilogy deals with such changes and, by its very intent, tries to open the eyes and minds of an unsuspecting audience seemingly content to live out their lives without giving these simple propositions so much as a passing thought. For some reason we find it easier to deal with things like slimy green lizards come to kill us all, or things that crawl into our bodies and take over our minds. We entertain the idea of intelligent insect populations so malevolent that they have nothing more in their brains than to eliminate humans from the universe. They don't need to have a reason.

Read on...and be changed. Read on...and understand that your world and its place in this system of planets near a small, yellow star is not the safe cocoon you may have thought it to be—you wish it to be.

Prologue

Space; frigid, silent darkness punctuated by a multitude of points of piercing light—light generated by the fury of hydrogen fusing to helium and other, heavier elements. Among all those brilliant pinpricks, more than half huddle inside vast girdles of gas, ice, mineral dust, and metal. In time these materials coalesce through a horrifying, violent and whirling dance into rocky planets, huge balls of gases, and globes of frozen gases, water ice, stone, and nickel-iron crystals. Some of the solid, stony-iron masses are pulverized into chunks that continue the ballet of the bullies, while others, out in the frozen fringe, wait quietly for something to come along that will jostle them enough to send them dashing headlong to join the fray, and the random violence erupts anew.

Some of these events are cyclical. Here, in our quiet little solar system, there appears to be one such cycle that occurs every thirty-two to thirty-five million years as we pass through the galactic plane, a transition we are now making, but other episodes can be triggered by the random, close passing of any massive object; dense clouds of dust and gas, blazars, planets ejected from their home systems with enough speed to wander free until they are trapped or forced to change direction by the cold grip of gravity, stars, or the burned out cinders of dead stars, and the list goes on.

That this cosmic clutter exists within our galaxy, indeed between the galaxies, too, is known with a high degree of surety. That these things make an occasional pass by or through our solar system is also well understood, but when they will come calling or when they have visited us and gone on their way, no one can say, with the notable exception of stellar data collected by the Hipparcos mission. It has to be mentioned also that the Hipparcos data only include information on selected visible stars coming our way or those that have already gone by—not the things that remain unseen, hidden from us. All that can be said is, it has happened in the past with devastating results. It will happen again. The passing of objects we know has occurred in the dimness of years past, but it often requires millions, even billions of years for the evidence of any such visitation to appear. When the signs of a chaos producing incident do make themselves known...it is too late, the chaos arrives full grown and the time of death follows not far behind—the Reaper spurs a silent, black steed into our midst and in his wake comes...THE RAIN...the hard rain.

Although what follows is a speculative fiction, it is rooted firmly in the soil of past, present, and future realities. It is a fiction that could easily become a living nightmare of hell while you are reading this, or it may not manifest itself for millennia. The only thing that can be said with certainty is, it will happen. The storm cloud will rise and the rain will fall. Are you ready? Should it arrive during your lifetime, do you have the information, the knowledge and the will you need to survive the advancing storm of hard, deadly rain

8

that gouges out huge holes in our little planet/spaceship and pulverizes entire regions of Earth? Will you be prepared to face the long, cold Winter that follows, one that lasts for years, perhaps centuries? Will your ancestors, should any of your progeny survive the Winter, be ready for the dangers of acid precipitation, deadly radiation, and the fierce, merciless storms that come with the Spring?

So, curl up in your favorite reading spot and get a preview of things to come. If you pay attention you will soon realize that this, though it is speculative fiction, is really a tale of things to come that are far from an imaginary flight to other worlds and that it can and will happen. Sorry, we have no idea of when. The dates given here in STORM CLOUD RISING are merely there to give the reader a sense for time-line. Perhaps sometime in the next few days the storm cloud will be seen rising. In the meantime, relax, but not too much, and do begin to prepare for THE RAIN.

Chapter 1

In the back yard of a large, rambling ranch house just north of highway 60 between Soccoro and Magdalena, New Mexico, Jeremy Stone, shivering in the sub-zero weather, presses his eye against the cup of the ocular, his pulse quickens and breathing becomes difficult. There can be no mistake, but what he is seeing is...is impossible. All his life, well, up until today, he has wanted to find one, but...but this sight is unreal, incredible, unbelievable. He steps back from the eyepiece and closes his eyes for a few minutes, then leans down to take another look. No, there is no mistake. It is no illusion. They are there. Tough to see, yes, but they are there.

I sure hope they're bright enough for my gear to track, he thinks.

Jeremy taps a series of numbers into the keypad he holds in his gloved hand and the system gives the signal that it has locked on the target and tracking has begun. Out in the computer shed, data recording and automated orbital reduction processing for later transmission to the International Astronomical Union also begins.

"Dad," he shouts at the intercom. "Dad, dad, come on out here...quick. Hurry."

Jeremy's father, Wendell Stone, pushes at the sliding glass door that opens onto the patio. He pulls his old woolen Navy watch cap, the ancient one his

11

wife keeps tossing out and he retrieves repeatedly from the trash, down to cover his ears, and trots over to the small observatory he and Jeremy built during the summer to house Jeremy's new two meter telescope and attendant computer systems.

"What? What is it, Jerry?"

"You're not gonna believe this, dad. Take...take a look," Jeremy says and steps away from the scope to make room for his father who, like Jeremy, is puffed out to almost double his girth in a quilted, down-filled jacket.

"Well, what do you know about that?" his father says. "You found one.

And it's a beauty, too. Have you checked the computer data to make sure it's not an existing—?"

"No, dad. Let your eyes adjust a little more and take another look— and yes, it's a new one— they're all new ones."

"They?" his father says, leaning back from the eyepiece with his eyes closed. "What do you mean, they?"

"Just look again, dad. Tell me how many you can see."

After another minute of resting his eyes in total darkness, Jeremy's father opens them and returns to the eyepiece. Jeremy watches impatiently as his father concentrates on trying to see with his old man's eyes what is trapped faintly in the eyepiece. His father gasps and almost staggers back from the scope.

"Well, I'll be damned," he says under his breath. "I'll be damned." He looks again and Jeremy figures it's probably to convince himself he's not seeing things because of Jeremy's suggestion in the plural. He pulls away from the eyepiece and looks at Jeremy who is standing, barely visible, in the dim red glow of the service light.

"Well?" Jeremy asks. He is aware his voice is oozing anticipation and excitement but, considering the circumstances, he doesn't care.

"I...I counted five of them. Is that what you saw?"

"No, Old Eyes. I saw...seven. Let's go to the computer room where we can enhance them on the screen and suppress Sirius so they're a lot easier to see. Besides, it's a heck of a lot warmer in there."

The two of them leave the dome and make their way across the crust of snow and ice that crunches and crackles under their boots to the small building adjacent to the observatory. Once inside and the door is closed against the bitter cold, Jeremy turns on the automated system's visual monitors.

"There. See? There are seven of them in a group. Oops, sorry...eight of them. They're so faint they get washed out against the glare of Sirius."

"Another Shoemaker-Levy 9?"

"No, dad. They're too far out to have been broken up by anything and, according to the track the system's calculated for them, they're on a hyperbolic path. It's their first and last visit to the sun."

"Oh, my...God. Quick, Jerry, connect to the Union and start transmitting your data. Wait 'til your mom hears about this...she'll flip. You're going to be famous, my man—if you get in before

13

anyone else does. Go, man...go, go, go."

"It's already running, dad. See? The receipt signal just came on."

They rush across the yard to the house for a cup of hot chocolate to toast Jeremy's discovery. In their hurry to celebrate, they don't notice the red warning light flashing news of a possible collision event.

* * *

12 January 2054: 1655 PST

"Hey, Sandy, I made it," Emery Klein called out as he came in through the door from the garage. "Where are ya, babe?" There was no answer. "Well, damn," he said to the air around him. He was accustomed to this empty home business. Their careers kept them on the move constantly, but...but sometimes it was frustrating, and this time she had promised she would be waiting with open arms, and there would be his favorite chocolate cake, plastered generously with extra thick fudge frosting, sitting on the dining room table. She even told him there would be candles on it, if she could find enough of them to cover the occasion...and she had picked out some filmy, flimsy black neglige for dessert.

Smart-ass woman.

But there was no cake and there was no Sandy, fully clothed or in a titillating, see-through toga of come hither black. "Comp."

"Yes, Dr. Klein?"

"Where's Mrs. Klein?"

The computer made the proper connections and

the wall screen in the living room came to life, fading from its usual Cascades scenery, and the image of his wife, standing against a backdrop of something that was decidedly not Los Angeles Metroplex, materialized.

"Hi, Em. I was just getting ready to get on the LA jump when you called. How did your trip go?" she said as she squeezed her way through a predominately Asian crowd loaded down with all manner of luggage, some even with hired carriers for their junk, all of them wearing that impatient don't-they-know-who-I-am look glued to their faces as they waited in long queues for jumpers to various locations around the world. "Find any good rocks?"

"The trip was great, if you like lots and lots of desert with hotter than hot days and cold...I mean frigid nights. Picked up a bunch of rocks, too, and they all look good. Perfect crusts on most of them, and I think we're going to be able to tie them in with the Allende fall of 1969—at least the same parent body, if not the same time. What with all the tracks and other evidence of people having been in the area where I found them, I can't figure out why no one else has ever come up with a few. Where are you?"

"Tokyo. I'll be home in about four hours, if the traffic at LAX isn't too bad. Wanna come pick me up?"

"It would be my pleasure, madame. Hey! Better than that, how about taking the shuttle and meeting me at Alpee's Tower? It'll save us from having to fight the local traffic and I am going to get my birthday din-din.

What were you doing in Tokyo, anyway?"

"Emergency meet with the Union reps. I'll tell you about it when I get to Alpee's, 'kay?"

"What's the matter with now?"

"Hushy...hushy, my love. Hushy and muy importante. That's why I couldn't let you know before I left. Bring me anything?"

"Yep. Really traditional Mexican, too. You're going to love it. Well, I think you will."

"Oh, yay. Okay, Em, gotta run or I'll miss the jump. See you at Alpee's, about ten, and I'll treat you to a great dinner as compensation for not being home like I said I would. Get us a table away from the maddening throng, huh? Oh, and happy birthday, old man."

"Fifty is not old," he said to the now blank screen. The screen faded back to the mountain scene Sandy loved and Emery unpacked the parrot he bought for her in Durango; a huge bird of hand-carved wood, and painted in garish greens, oranges, yellows, purples, blues and the deepest of blacks— an incredibly ugly thing that he thought would take a place of honor. It would probably find its spot perched on top of that equally hideous glass pillar objet d'art—couldn't call it anything else without waxing obscene—she brought back from Paris a couple of months ago. The pillar was supposed to be a sculpture of a nude holding a platter over her head, but it looked to Emery more like a twisted, surrealistic representation of a gnarled, grotesque tree trunk sporting exaggerated buttocks and ballooning breasts— the only recognizable things about it. The damned thing had to weigh in at

16

around three hundred kilos.

The bird was sure to be a big hit with Sandy. As for the load of stones he lugged back from La Zona del Silencio, that was still up for grabs. Crude field tests strongly suggested they were recently fallen meteoritic material and his instincts told him he had been lucky on this trip but, until he got them under the new super-microprobe and mass spectrum analyzer in the lab for a more thorough analysis, who could say whether they were recent visitors or had been out there in the sand for a few thousand years? They were, without doubt, beautiful stony meteorites, carbonaceous and sporting an impressive array of well-formed chondrules, if they weren't the same, did a good job of mimicking the Allende fall samples. He was sure they were related, if not from the same event. He shrugged off his disappointment over not finding Sandy at home, neglige or not, and headed for the shower to flush the remainder of the desert out of his pores.

What could be so hushy that she couldn't use the grid to tell me what was going on?

At least it was a Monday evening, so Alpee's wouldn't be packed. From the image on the screen, Sandy hadn't appeared to be her usual, happy self, either. She appeared to be somewhat preoccupied...and nervous. Sandy was never nervous. Preoccupied, yes...but never nervous. Nervousness was something that had not been included in her genetic makeup and it would take a lot to bring such a foreign emotion to the surface so that it could be seen as well as heard. After his shower he would contact the Union to see if there were any new bulletins, just in case it wasn't so hushy after all.

* * *

Emery pulled into a charging stall in Alpee's parking garage at about 9:30 and hooked up. There was no need for him to go anywhere for Sandy. She would be shuttled directly to the restaurant right after the pad was cleared of people and their packages. Whatever luggage she may have brought with her would be sent straight to the security receiver at the house. She always traveled light, so there should be no problem.

Alpee's Tower, located about five kilometers offshore, was built on a substructure of twenty huge, floating pylons, similar in concept to the old offshore oil rigs, but much more complex and on a scale that dwarfed all the other structures around it. Automated anchor reels and high volume, fast-ballasting provided for a stable platform, come future quakes or high water. Since the last big quake in '39, buildings in the LA Metro were restricted to ten stories with stringent guidelines regarding base size versus height. Several towered structures went up immediately after the quakes on existing but no longer used oil rigs to help make up for the lost office space in the LA basin during the clean-up and rebuilding of the regions that hadn't slid into the sea, but none were a match for Alpee's. The restaurant at the top of the hundred story structure was considered the finest on the west coast, providing a breathtaking view of the LA Metro's sprawling and constantly outward crawling boundaries. In addition, the restaurant kept a menu unparalleled in its selections and constantly upward crawling prices. Pure class was the only way to describe Alpee's.

He was right about the place not being stuffed with bodies. Hardly anyone was in the restaurant. He told the maitre d' he wanted a table for two as far from anyone as he could get and that he would be celebrating his birthday; that little comment would secure them a complimentary bottle of good champagne and a frosted cupcake with a candle jammed into its middle. It would also bring a couple of waiters to warble the birthday song for him—off key and filled with abrasive dissonance.

He was ushered to a small table on the western side against the windows where the lights of the Tower playfully bounced and scattered off Pacific waves as they stacked up at the continental shelf and headed toward the beach. If it weren't for the lights from the various offshore structures dancing in the undulating ocean, the night would have been completely black, the thin sliver of the moon having set just a little while before he got to the restaurant's garage and an evening overcast had taken its place. Ah, perfect, he mused. Whatever it was that had taken Sandy to Tokyo had not appeared anywhere in the IAU's site and, oddly, there were no new bulletins posted from the sixth of the month on. Strange, he thought. Traffic of all sorts always littered the boards, but he found nothing—nothing at all.

Emery looked up from the menu plate

embedded in the tabletop and saw the maitre d' heading his way with a dark green bottle in a chrome ice bucket that dangled from his left hand, and Sandy in tow on his right. She looked tired. Tired and worried...and she had a security attaché case cuffed to her wrist, a heavy metal one reserved for top secret documents and diamonds.

What the hell is going on here?

"Hi, Em," she said as she settled down at the table, her voice filled with a nervousness he could touch. "You picked a good spot."

"I didn't pick it, he did," Emery said, casting a thumb at the retreating maitre d'. "So, what's going on here...and what's with the attaché case? Or should I say 'portable safe?'"

Sandra Klein leaned forward over the table and spoke in a hushed voice as if she were holding a secret she wanted to tell and all the people in Alpee's were spies straining to hear it. "Flux rate for cometary material has gone up several levels of magnitude during the last six days," she said, her voice held low and conspirative in tone. "Reports of multiple sightings are coming in from all over the globe."

"This isn't a 'The sky is falling!' thing, is it?"

"Not hardly. All rock solid observers and most with direct links to the system so their observations can be checked directly."

"You said there are multiples?"

"Mm-hmm. Three, seven, ten in a group," she said as she unreeled a length of security cable from the case so she would be able to move a bit more freely. "As usual, most of the data is flowing in

20

from the amateurs, but they, the potentates of government wisdom, have seized control of all the available major observatories to analyze the problem and determine what it may mean."

"Cause?"

"No one has any good answers. A number of people, some of them even close to respectable, offered up the normal stuff—you know the routine; gravity waves; cycling through the galactic disc; passing gravity well; bow shock from a fast moving object, like a blazar, perhaps, but there really is no way to know. Whatever it was happened several millions, maybe billions of years ago and, until these things began appearing, there was no evidence—"

"Yeah, yeah, I know. Nemesis, or Planet X, or any other such nonsense. Just wait until the UFO gang and conspiracy clods get hold of this. The rag papers will be filled with more crap than their regular fare. Any of them dangerous?"

"Some of them in the eighty-five percent bracket, but no, not yet...but...but there are so many, Em. Most are highly inclined and won't pass near our orbital track, but there are some—enough—on and close to the ecliptic that are going to cross with the sort of proximity that'll make anyone nauseous. Nothing beyond a two on the scale—yet. But...but potential collisions in the belt might kick some of your ordinary rocks around enough to create a second set of threats as well as breaking up some of the comets, and disrupting the tracks the observatories will have already established for them. That will generate a third threat from pieces with unknown paths. The orbits they have so far are all indicating their origin to have been beyond the Kuiper Belt's limit—somewhere in the inner Oort.

Quite a few of them appear to be of substantial size. Most of the orbital vectors they've been able to pin down have been determined to be hyperbolic, so, once they've gone by, we won't be seeing them again, and some are going to pass the sun close enough to be drawn in, but there are enough—"

"Yeah, but hyperbolic tracks also mean high cosmic velocities. Comets from that far out always move fast. Lots of energy, even in the small stuff. So, we have cosmic billiards, again. Oort orbits are tenuous to start with and it wouldn't have taken much to knock things around and prompt their fall in. The best we can hope for is that most of those that have our name on them will detonate in the upper atmosphere. What's being called substantial size?"

"Four—five kilometers. Some have been tentatively identified as being in the ten kilometer range, and some may be even bigger. All of them are low-albedo objects, so they're hard to see until they start outgassing. Radar sweeps are being organized to make sure we cover as large a portion of sky as we can in as short a time as possible."

"There's a whole bunch of sky out there, Sandy. The sizes starting at four kilometers? That's substantial, all right, and so much for high altitude detonations. Even a rubble pile at five kilometers will make it down to impact. Anybody have any ideas about what can be done? We're still years away from being able to deflect anything

22

threatening, especially after the budget cuts of '29 and the dismantling of several key programs by the wise politicians we entrust our world to—in spite of the Posner Protocols, I hasten to add—politicians who don't know the difference between meteoroids and hemorrhoids," Emery said, his voice mirroring the tension he felt in hers. "Have they set up any sort of action plan...on the off-chance we do get smacked by one or more of the biggies?"

"We were advised that there is a program in place to keep the public from reacting—from panic, you know. Nothing beyond that...and no one said anything about what that program is or how it will be implemented. I'll be finding out about that when I get back to work this week. Maybe as early as tomorrow. That's what's in the attaché case—speaking of which, I have to stop by the office on the way home to put it in the safe. Do you mind the little detour? Security's waiting for me, so it won't take long."

"Aha, they thought it was so important and sensitive that they opted to hand carry it, rather than send it through the system, huh?"

"Looks that way, yeah," she said and nodded toward her extra appendage. "So, do you mind the side trip?"

"Would it make any difference if I did?"

"Not in the slightest, unless you'd like sleeping with this attaché case between us."

"We'll go to the office first."

* * *

General Abram Stoker awoke to the grating tone of the security alarm sounding from his ear implant. His first, semiconscious response was to carelessly swat at it, as if it were a gnat or mosquito buzzing near his ear, until he was awake enough to recognize what it was. They installed the infernal device nine years ago, when he was assigned to the program, and he, still not accustomed to its presence, continued to think of it as a nuisance, an intrusion on what little privacy he previously knew.

"Stoker here," he said softly so he wouldn't awaken his wife who lay sleeping peacefully at his side.

"Voice print cleared. Full ID required for incoming priority message," the small voice in his ear said.

Priority? What the hell?

He rolled quietly from under the covers, slipped on his robe, automatically shoved his feet into slippers parked beside the bed and shuffled down the hall to his den. He awakened to that blasted contraption four or five times a month, usually for a system test, but this was the first priority message in all those years. He closed the outer door and barred it, then slid the security door closed and listened for the telltale snap of the automatic locks that sealed the room off from the rest of the world.

Stoker walked over to a bookcase against the far wall and pressed the back of a book, appropriately titled The Final Days, and the case swivelled around on hinges in the floor and ceiling, revealing a full console of blinking lights, maps, and several screens. He pressed his right hand on a glass plate on the console and his right eye up to an eyepiece protruding from the face of the vertical panel.

"ID accepted. Room scan secure," the irritating little voice said.

One of the screens came to life, displaying briefly the Great Seal of the United States, then faded to just two words flashing insistently on the screen. The two words Stoker hoped he would never see, at least not as long as he was charged with responsibility for this damnable program. How many innocent citizens am I going to have to sequester or eliminate before this is under control, he wondered?

I guess it doesn't really matter. It's my baby and there must be a good reason for them to run up the flag now.

The message, he knew, came straight from the Whitehouse. The command emanated directly from the fingertip of the person who had the needed power and clearance to push the button, and the only person who possessed the authority to do the pressing was—the president, herself.

"LAUNCH LAZARUS," flashed on the screen in a dozen languages. "Well, shit," Stoker said in an automatic reflex. The sound of his own voice startled him, then his fingers began savagely tapping codes into the system as they glided in a well-rehearsed pattern over the keyboard. The only consolation he had in all this was the morbid knowledge that his counterparts in all the large,

Project Lazarus participating countries around the world, were going through the same thing, having the same thoughts in most cases. This was not something anyone could take lightly, no matter how callous they might be. Clandestine teams were already being mobilized in smaller, non-participating states without their governments' knowledge, and people everywhere were going to begin disappearing or turning up dead within a few minutes of his response to that two word message; the majority of them would be civilians who were guilty of nothing more than seeing something they shouldn't have seen.

Launch Lazarus. Silence to keep the masses ignorant and may they forever remain so, he thought, and chewed at his inner cheek until it was raw and hurting.

"This is a damned doomsday program—worse than anything out of the fifties," he said when they assigned him to Project Lazarus. Now, it appeared, their proposed doomsday scenario was upon them. What, he wondered, had triggered it? He logged in his acknowledgment code, then staggered sleepily over to his desk where he poured out an eight ounce glass of cognac, sat down and began sipping with the intent of becoming quite drunk. There could be no doubt about the importance of the program, but it left a vacant, lonely feeling deep in his gut and he was determined to fill that void with something...numbing.

LAUNCH LAZARUS...shit.

* * *

Sandra Klein poked her head in the doorway to her husband's small office, the place where he rode herd on what he referred to as The Cosmic Rock Quarry, and cleared her throat to get his attention.

"Hey, Em, want to have lunch with me at the Dog Pit today?"

He had his back turned to the door and, at the sound of her voice, nearly dropped the delicate thin section he was holding up to the light.

"Huh? What?"

"Dog Pit. Lunch. You and me—we go, yes?"

"Oh, yeah...sure. Sounds good to me," he said, and put the section slide down on his desk. "Heard anything about...?"

"Sh-h-h."

"Sh-h-h?"

"Come on, I'm starving. Think I'll have one of their foot-longs with sauerkraut, mustard and onions. What about you?"

"O' ye of the iron gut. No way, lady. I think I'll have something more digestible...like a polish with chilli and cheese."

"Oh, yuk. I thought I was supposed to be the one with an iron gut.

Come on, let's go."

* * *

For a day in the middle of January, she didn't feel cold and the sky was as clear as it ever got over

27

the city. Sandra Klein laid claim to a small, round table with an expanded metal top located near the street corner and out of the shadow of the tiny building, barely larger than a good-sized broom closet, called the Dog Pit, while her husband went to the walk-up window to place their order. She felt worry, fear, and something stronger than anger permeating every cell in her body. What right, she thought, did the government have to do what it was doing? The meeting, long, loud, and argument-filled, finally settled down to everyone agreeing to do what the government was demanding of them—keep their mouths shut and continue to study the situation. The not-so-well veiled threats had a lot to do with that, she thought.

Emery Klein came away from the window carrying a little red plastic tray, too small for its cargo, filled with messy-looking hot dogs, two large drinks and a stack of the required supply of napkins in one hand. His other hand was laid over the top of the napkins to keep them from blowing away in the wind that continued to stiffen into the daily afternoon offshore.

Sandra watched him in a new way today, appreciating her man as never before. A tall man, carrying the slight paunch a fellow of his age usually develops but, otherwise, he was lean and muscular from years of scouring deserts in far away places with unpronounceable names in search of his precious rocks. His face, gaunt, looking as if it had been hacked from solid granite, showed an intelligence and gentleness in defiance of the tough-guy ruggedness in its foundation. His curly hair and

28

full beard were totally white now and stood out in shocking contrast to his perpetually deep tan. He was still the man who had attracted her when they were both juniors in the university and he was still the only one who could turn her on with a simple glance from those intense blue eyes—quite probably the only one who could live with her little, well, sometimes large idiosyncracies. God, how she loved that man and there seemed to be an urgency about it now. Things were changing rapidly...and out of their control. She wasn't certain how the new conditions were going to affect them, but she did know they would affect them at a personal level.

"Hey, Sandy, give me a hand here, would you?" he said, and set the tray down on the table, while she protected the napkin stack. "Now, want to tell me what was behind the 'sh-h-h' back there?"

"They probably have the whole university...um, bugged by now.

That's the right word, isn't it? Bugged, like when somebody's listening to what goes on without anyone else knowing it?"

"Uh, yeah...it is." An eyebrow arched. "Who would want to listen to a bunch of stodgy old professors rambling on about their pet this and that...and why?"

"We had our meeting over what was in the attaché case this morning.

A couple of VIP-type government reps, accompanied by a batch of black- suited guys with short hair and dark glasses, presented us with their requirements—their demands is more like it. And the guys in the black suits...? They all looked so much alike that they could have been extruded from the same tube. Eerie."

"And...?"

"And they're imposing a kind of limited, carefully targeted martial law on us and certain segments of society. You'll probably be getting your notice this afternoon. Remember the scare in thirty-nine, when 2036 JM7 missed us by a thousand kilometers?"

"Yeah...who could forget? And not even the LSSTs saw it coming until it was too late. Two kilometers of solid nickel-iron going by so close you could reach out and touch the damned thing. For months afterward you could see people looking up once in a while when they were walking, as if they thought it realized it had missed and turned around to finish the job.

And how about Apophis? Surprised everyone when it came through and missed the keyhole by an arm's length. Then the deflection attempt went sour and it slapped us in the southern tip of Argentina in forty-two? Very embarrassing for all the agencies that said it would miss by two lunar radii."

"Mm-hmm, well, the impact of Apophis, along with the nasty changes in the climate afterward and the incredibly close pass of JM7 are the things that caused them to get moving on a series of projects to preserve our infrastructure and knowledge base in case something similar but bigger had us in its sights. I guess...I guess they got around to realizing that what we've been telling them all along was a lot more than a scare tactic to get more funding. The lip service they gave us after Shoemaker-Levy 9 and their penny-sized allowances for improved observations didn't help much, but JM7 made them get serious.

"This increased flux rate triggered their new program into action and we're all subject to a different set of rules." She took another bite of her hot dog and continued with her mouth full, "All the major players have been working on several installations scattered around the world in the equatorial zone and the colony sites on the moon and Mars since forty-five. Were you aware that Zubrin City at Olympus has over a thousand people in it and the JAXA Pavonis station has more than that?"

"What?"

"That's right, and that's why the European consortium and NASA got their new mega-boost beasts. More than four thousand are living in the main colonies now, when we all thought there were no more than five or six hundred. Several of the so-called large satellite launches and supply lifts from here and other pads around the world weren't what they said they were—what they let out for public consumption. LC-3 in Plato has even more people in it than the two Martian colonies put together and they're set up to accept a couple of thousand more at any time. The Japanese, Russians, Chinese, and Indians have been even more energetic than we have. They've been working on deep, subsurface habitats and major launch facilities on the moon and Mars continuously since twenty-forty."

"Well, bless their devious little hearts. I'm glad they did it, but how did they manage to keep this

31

program of theirs so quiet...and what's the name they gave to their little project?"

"Lazarus. They kept it quiet by using things that have become worn out with time, like satellite launches and maintenance flights. Nobody paid any attention—not even those of us who should have known better.."

"Lazarus? Oh, now, that's cute. Sort of a preemptive triage, huh?"

"I didn't think of it that way, but I suppose you could call it that. It gives me the creeps, Em. Look out there on the street. People. People just like us, going about their business and unaware that their own government has already decided their fate. You die—we don't."

"Not just like us, Sandy. They don't know what we do—and that worries me. How about you? You think an impact is imminent?"

"I don't know. I really...don't know, yet."

"Well, I do. I took the data I could get my hands on—wasn't much, I have to admit—and I've been running a series of simulations based on what we think we know at the moment. The chance of a major impact in the next ten years is better than eighty-nine percent, using just the paltry info I could dig up, and the multiple impacts from smaller chunks scenario ranks even higher. Within ten years, maybe less, it'll be raining rocky ice balls and other junk. It'll be a storm that could easily last, according to the numbers I get, a hundred or more years."

Sandra Klein sat quietly for a moment, giving all he said a chance to sink in. What it meant to her

32

was that major impactors, just one or two big ones, would bring on the Long Winter and its attendant ice age. Apophis came close to doing it by itself. Add to that the more than considerable volcanic and seismic activity around the world that would be generated, all of it exacerbating the problems people would be facing, and you would be looking at nothing less than survival of the fittest. All that material going into the upper atmosphere would measurably increase the pall of darkness enshrouding the Earth—sealing off the surface from the life-supporting energy of the sun.

Multiple impacts from the smaller pieces would ensure that no place on Earth would be safe from local and regional destruction. People would be dying by the millions, maybe billions, from the effects of impacts, and coastal cities would be inundated by gigantic waves in the first part of what could only be called the coming storm. Starvation as the food chain collapsed and freezing from the long term effects would soon follow. A breakdown in the social order and technical substructures that kept things running was inevitable and would probably happen pretty fast. It was sobering, depressing, frightening, even maddening. She and her Em were caught up in it on what appeared to be the wrong side of the fence. How much more pleasant would it be to remain ignorant of such things?

"Em...you have some time on the books, don't you?"

"A couple of weeks—maybe a little more. Why?"

"I'm going out to the new VLA tomorrow

33

morning. Want to come with me?"

"Aha! Desert. Flat. Rocks. Sure, why not? Why the VLA?"

"You forgot to mention cold—very cold."

"Oh, yeah, so I did. Brr-r-r, cold rocks. So, why the VLA?"

"Excuse, my slow genius."

"Excuse? Excuse for what?"

"An excuse to talk to Mr. Jeremy Stone. He lives just off Highway 60 about halfway to Magdalena. He was the first amateur in the States to report a multiple sighting to the Union—a high probability impact group, a string of eight, exceeding eighty-five percent—and I want to see how he's being treated."

"When did he make his report?"

"On the tenth."

"He may not even be there now."

"What makes you say that?"

"He may already have been scooped up and dragged off, or whatever they plan to do with witnesses. A kind of witness protection plan where they're protecting the public and themselves from the witnesses."

"I don't believe that, and I still need to know."

"Uh-huh. You could get us in a lot of trouble by taking a personal interest beyond the physics of this event, you know."

"I understand that...but I have to know," she said, and she meant it.

The whole business gnawed at her viscera like a ball of hungry, vicious worms. How, she thought, could the government, any government, in good conscience, do this to its own people? Oh, she knew the reasons underlying their program, of course, and they were right. At the intellectual level she could see and appreciate the choices that were going to have to be made, but emotionally the idea made her sick—she just couldn't compartmentalize the two ideas, and knowing who was making the decisions infuriated her more. Millions were going to die outright in the first wave of impactors that Emery was sure were coming and millions—billions more in the long run, especially those who didn't understand the nature of what was happening; the hell-in-a-freezer and starvation that would follow the first major strikes, while those making the rules slept happily in their cozy little hideouts down south.

"Okay. Okay. I only have two Friday classes and I can get Perkins to sit in for me. If we can get back here before Monday morning, I won't have to use any of my time and I won't have to tell anyone what I'm doing.

Probably better that way—not notifying anyone, I mean."

At that moment a shadow passed over their table and they were flanked by two burly looking guys with crew-cuts, wearing dark suits and cheap sunglasses. They looked like they just stepped off the screen from an old vid she recalled seeing when she was ten years old. She couldn't remember the name of it, but it was very funny, whatever it was. This wasn't funny in the least. Now she felt cold, and it had nothing to do with the weather.

"Pardon us, Mrs. Klein, Mr. Klein, but we

would rather not have you out here in public any more than is absolutely necessary. You understand."

"We were just having lunch, for God's sake."

"There's a cafeteria for that, Mr. Klein."

"Yeah, right. Have you eaten any of that crap yet? Obviously not...you're still alive."

Chapter 2

Emery Klein switched to manual mode and steered the rental car they picked up in Soccoro off the highway's automated track. He followed a dirt road, nothing more than a broken trail through the patchy snow, to the north.

According to the fellow at the rental agency, they would find the Stone's residence about ten kilometers from the highway. The rental agent also told them that Mrs. Stone had rented a car from him ten days before to make a trip up to Albequerque to visit her ailing mother and had returned it early on the fifteenth. Mr. Stone picked her up and he seemed edgy, maybe even angry, when he came into the office for her, the agent said. He added that they weren't the only ones interested in the Stone's. He told them that a couple of what he referred to as "goons" had been in the previous day asking a lot of questions about the Stone family, too. Emery Klein wondered what kind of mess they were about to get into. He was still wondering about that when they crested a small knoll and the Stone's house came into view.

The house, a low and expansive structure, partly brick, partly cement block, and some wood with a full width front porch that was covered and enclosed in darkly tinted, double-paned glass, was typical of homes that grew in the southwestern high deserts in spurts from whatever materials were available when an addition was made. Behind the house stood a large, professional looking dome and two big wind generators. On either side of the door leading to the front porch were two men in matching, three-quarter length, overstuffed, quilted jackets, their 12ga. shotguns pointed menacingly in the direction of the car and unerringly following their approach.

"Some welcoming party," he said as he turned into the drive. "They probably think we're more of those, what did the guy back there call them, goons?"

"Yeah...whatever. You get out first."

"Why?"

"Because, if they see your dainty, feminine frame first, maybe they'll point those nasty looking things in some other direction."

"Right," she said and stepped out of the car onto the ice encrusted drive. "Hi, there. We're from the Cal Western University Astrono—"

"You just stop right where you are, ma'am, and explain why you're out here," the elder of the two said. He raised the shotgun to a more useable and threatening level.

"We've come to talk to you about the report you made to the IAU," Emery Klein said from the other side of the car. "Are you Mr. Jeremy Stone?"

"No. Jerry's my son here. My name's Wendell."

The shotguns remained at the ready and pointed in their direction. "Pretty cold out here, Wendell. Would you mind if we come in?"

Sandra Klein asked.

"Oh...yeah. Yeah, sure. Sorry about all this, but

the fellows who were out here yesterday weren't what you could call friendlies."

The shotguns lowered and the door to the porch opened, revealing a thin, small woman holding a rifle with scope. The weapon was almost bigger than she was, but it also appeared she knew what to do with it. She sent a semi-friendly but suspicious smile in their direction and draped the sling of the rifle over her shoulder, the rifle's butt nearly dragging on the porch planking as she turned and moved into the house.

Wendell Stone and his son waited until the Kleins passed through the door, then followed with their shotguns lowered, but still ready to use.

Emery Klein felt uneasy and he was amazed by how calmly his wife appeared to be taking all of it. Why is this family so on edge? Yesterday's visitors, I'll bet.

"Have a seat there at the table while Lolly gets the coffee. Looks like you folks could use it. Got some ID you can show me?"

Jeremy Stone went into the living room with both of the shotguns and set them on a glassed in rack on the wall by the fireplace, but didn't lock it. Lolly Stone leaned her rifle against the wall by the kitchen unit and poked at a few buttons on the panel, while Wendell Stone drew a chair out from the large, round, dining room table, spun it around backwards and straddled it, his arms crossed over the top of its short back. Emery and Sandy Klein handed him their university ID plates. He looked them over, glanced up to compare faces with photos, then asked, "So, what is it you want to know?"

"What did they tell you, Wendell?" Sandra Klein said.

"They told us that we were not to say anything to anyone about what Jerry saw. They said it was of the utmost importance. They said we would be jeopardizing matters of national security if we revealed what we saw and they told us that what we saw was a new type of...satellite—top secret stuff, they said."

"And you believed them?"

"Not for an instant. Doesn't take much of a rocket scientist to know the difference between a comet beginning to outgas and nice, shiny, new satellites. Besides, the orbital data Jerry recorded made that impossible, unless they were launching them from somewhere beyond Pluto. New satellites, my ass."

"Did they say anything that sounded like a threat—beyond the breach in national security?" Emery Klein asked.

"Oh, yeah. Everything they said had a threat of some kind nailed to it.

Not that they said anything out loud and clear, you know...but the threat was there anyway." Wendell Stone's eyes narrowed and he leaned across the table toward them. "If we weren't so well-known around this area, I don't think we'd be here right now, and I don't think it's going to be too much longer before they come back out here. You know, to pay us a visit, plant some surveillance gear, and turn us into rats in a cage...or do something worse—if they haven't already done it."

40

"Oh, Wendell, your paranoia's swinging free in the wind again," Lolly Stone said as she set coffee cups and spoons on the table for everyone. "Why would they do that? We haven't done anything."

"You don't know the government the way I do, Lolly. Why do you suppose they put security seals on Jerry's observatory—and not the ordinary tape stuff, but seals you can't break? I don't doubt for a minute they have our communications covered, too, so don't you even think of calling your mom, or anyone else for that matter. The less they know about what we're doing, the better."

* * *

On the highway again and headed for the new VLA, Emery and Sandra Klein sat in stunned silence for several minutes. She couldn't believe all she heard at the Stone's house. The government's goons told them they would be prosecuted and subject to imprisonment for up to ten years if any of them were to talk about what Jeremy had seen. Although it didn't vary much from what they said in the meeting at the university, it seemed worse somehow when it came to private citizens who didn't owe any of their support to federal programs and funding.

When she finally rid herself of her initial shock, she said, "Is it possible that something like this is actually happening here in the United States?"

"Not just possible, Sandy. Those idiots have been making decisions for the sake of the ignorant masses for centuries. Why should it change now?

And I guarantee you it's not just happening here, this is going on all over the world."

"Well, yes, but put the parents in prison and Jeremy in the government's care? Ten years?"

"Government's care doesn't mean what it sounds like, either. The conditions would be a little different, maybe, but he would be in prison, too. I don't believe these people are going to be allowed to remain free for much longer, anyway. And I don't think the government will bother with the prosecution end of it. Surveillance or not, the Stones represent a potential threat to whatever this Lazarus thing is intended to accomplish—and, I remind you, so do we and a lot of other people. We're already in a heap of trouble, Sandy, and what we just did, if they find out about it, will get us locked up right along with them. For all I know, they may lock us up anyway—just to be sure there aren't any leaks in the plumbing."

"No. They...they wouldn't do that."

"Yes, they would, and they probably will. I hope you have a plausible reason for us being out here."

"I made an appointment with Hoffman to discuss something I've been working on for the last six months. While I'm there you can go scrounging around for rocks. We'll be about five hours, maybe a little more, and he said we could spend the night in the on-site housing. Is that good enough?"

"It'll have to be. Don't mention any of this to Hoffman, either. If he brings it up, okay, but, whatever you do, keep your input general. I...I think I've figured out what this Lazarus thing is about.

It's quite logical and it does make a lot of sense—if you can keep your emotions out of it, that is. I think they want to keep the technological base intact. Above all, they need to avoid any sort of general panic. If the people go nuts—and who could blame them?—it would interfere with their plans. Anyway, if they're successful, once we've been hit as much as we're going to be, they can come up out of their cozey little hiding places and begin reconstructing whatever is left—I don't think that's going to be much, though. Most of it won't be salvageable after a century or more of being pushed around in the ice."

"That's a pretty big plan, isn't it? I mean, how do they do all that without anyone finding out what's going on."

"They told you at the meeting. First, they move all of the key people who are in a position to do what will need to be done to safe places around the equatorial belt here on Earth and to Lunar and Martian colonies like they said. Then they move in and take over all the information outlets that deal with making scientific findings public and everybody reads from a script that people like us will be forced into writing for them to keep the general populace in the dark and believing they're safe—until the absolute, last minute."

"That's thousands of places and hundreds of thousands of people, Em. And those who get locked up will have friends, relatives—jobs. How would they explain that?"

"They have more than enough goons available to do the job, I'm sure. For those who disappear, I'll give you ten to one they have a mix and match package of ready-made stories with all the evidence needed to support them."

"And coming out to do the rebuilding? It...it'll be a few generations before anything like that would be possible. You said it yourself. The actual impact danger could last for a century, the dust and ash from it all could easily hang in the atmosphere another hundred years plus, the acid rains that will come, not to mention seismic and volcanic activity that will be stirred up...and who knows how long it will take for enough ozone to build up again to bring the UV levels down once all that is over?"

"That's true, but you can think of their safe places as big, self- contained, hidden colonies here on Earth. All those qualified to be shipped to those places will teach subsequent generations and keep things going until it's safe enough to come out of their holes and rebuild the world. Their world. The way they want it. I also need to tell you that we aren't on their list of the chosen. Imagine. Lazarus."

She was imagining, and getting more worried and angrier by the minute. How dare they do this to us?

"What about Bobby, Morgan...and the kids?" she said.

"I'm going to have to talk to her about all this, and soon," he replied. "I just haven't figured out how."

* * *

17 January 2054: 0930 EST

"Ladies and gentlemen, Operation Roundup is set to commence on 1 February. Some emergency tidying up is going on now, but that doesn't concern you. You are to have all your Sector Chiefs briefed and prepared by the twenty-fifth of this month. I want a state of readiness report from each of you in my files by 1500 hours tomorrow. I remind you that you now have a choice of three camps in each sector, instead of the two described in the original Lazarus Operations Manual. Southwestern and Northeastern Sectors, you now have five. You will all receive notices detailing where these new facilities are located and what their recommended population capacities are.

"Preliminary lists of those to be sequestered will be in your systems by the twenty-first. I want you to use discretion in separating family units, but if it is deemed necessary, do not hesitate to do so. There are to be no mistakes and no delays. All the people on your lists have been advised, using the standard cover stories, of their position and responsibility. They are under observation now, just in case any of them decide to talk anyway. As I said, the most sensitive cases are already being picked up. Any questions?" Stoker surveyed the group of a hundred and twenty specially picked and trained Region Bosses in the hall and sensed some doubt in the faces of fully a quarter of them. He wondered if his uncertainty and concern showed as much as theirs.

Can we really pull this thing off? Time will tell, I suppose. It's a damned good thing that we'll be

45

writing the history.

Lazarus was a monumental undertaking, riddled with places where errors, misjudgments, and simple misunderstandings could spring up as full grown weeds on a putting green and mutate into total jungles of disaster in less than a heartbeat. Stoker shuddered at the thought that, if it began to unravel, he would be left standing in the middle of the mess with nowhere to hide and no cover story that anyone would believe.

Launch Lazarus.

There were no questions, though he knew there should have been some.

These people are as intimidated by Lazarus as the poor souls they're going to throw into their concentration camps will be.

"Gunny," Stoker said to the gunnery sergeant standing by the door as the last of the group of Region Bosses filed out. "I want to see the ISA people—now—in my office."

* * *

The Internal Security Agency, the original designers of Project Lazarus, grew from a small office full of computer geeks, hackers and end-of-the- world gamesters, to an entity numbering in the thousands with unimaginable power. It was still run by geeks, hackers and gamesters, but now it had the full backing of the government and walk-in access to the Whitehouse, something even Stoker's three stars didn't give him. The recent discoveries of impending doom added greatly to their prestige as a

46

family of modern day prophets and oracles but, to Stoker, they were still nothing more than digital geeks.

"There are two things I want to know," Stoker said to the three men seated on the other side of his desk. One of the men was preoccupied with a game pad and another was poking around in a small box with a miniature probe. Only the man in the center appeared to be paying any attention at all. Geeks. "Number one, do we have any idea yet when the first one is going to hit?"

"Not the specific date and time," the apparent speaker for the group said, "but, yes, we know. It's going to arrive in the last half of June in sixty- one. It is a small one, about three hundred meters in diameter, and, according to our sources, it appears to be a rubble pile. MC Pavonis launched a probe to verify the structure of that one—yesterday, I believe."

"Seven and a half years? That's a lot sooner than the original estimate, isn't it?"

"They're refining their data by the hour, General Stoker. They tell us they'll know the date, time and probable location of the strike within two weeks. Their best guess now is around the twenty-fourth and it will come down somewhere in the mid-southern Pacific. If it succeeds in getting through the atmosphere—everyone doubts it will—it's not big enough to generate a dangerous wave, well, not dangerous at a distance. Odds are that the object will disintegrate high in the atmosphere. The one following it, though, is of some concern because it appears to be about three kilometers in diameter and much more solidly built. It will hit two days later a bit north of Panama and will create some global problems. Anything beyond those two is still being studied. Why? Is the great General Stoker getting the jitters so soon?"

"No," he said, though he knew it was an outright lie. Stoker didn't like the snide tone of the middle geek one bit.

"And, what was the second thing you wanted to know?"

"Has my family been included on the relocation list?"

"I can't answer that."

"Can't...or won't?"

"I can't. Believe it or not, General, that kind of information isn't available to us. If it will make you feel any better, none of us have any information about the lists, and most of us have families we would like to see taken care of. Dodging falling rocks for who-knows-how-long, then sitting out a hundred year winter in the open is not my idea of fun."

"I suppose that's a fair enough answer," Stoker replied. "I can tell you this much, if the welcome mat is not out for us, and we don't fly south with the rest of the snow-birds, we are all going to be thoroughly pissed puppies and there will be hell to pay coming out the other side. That I can guarantee."

* * *

17 January 2054: 0850 MST

48

"Excuse me, Mrs. Hathaway, but we have to confirm receipt. Please push the yellow button with your right thumb."

Roberta Hathaway placed her thumb on the button and pushed firmly. The courier company's system instantly searched the available information, confirmed her identity as the rightful recipient and recorded the transaction for later download to their database.

"Thank you, ma'am," the young man said. "Have a nice day. Uh, as nice a day as you can have in this blizzard." He made a broad wave at the snow driving against the windows of the Hathaway's enclosed porch.

Roberta Hathaway laughed and keyed the door open. The courier turned and vanished into a howling wind that was building meter high drifts against the northern walls of the house.

Thank goodness for couriers, she thought, but why would Dad send me a package without calling first? By a private service, no less. Strange.

She tore the outer covering from the box with the patience of a small child opening a birthday present. Under the wrapping, she found a security sealed box with a palm pad on its side.

A security box, too?

She laid her hand on the pad and the thing popped open to reveal a handwritten note, a small vid chip, a large manila envelope stuffed full of something, and a container of oily-looking fluid. The note was in her father's hand.

He never writes notes. What's going on here?

"Hi, Bobby," the note began, "I want you to play this chip, but make sure you've disconnected the vid from your com and comp systems first. It might be a good idea to disconnect everything else from the grid, too. Pay very close attention to the vid and commit everything in it to your fabulous memory. Be sure to play the chip through three times, even if you think you remember everything in it the first time, which I'm sure you will. It's been programmed to clean itself and the vid system after the third viewing. Then reconnect your vid to the systems so you don't attract any attention by being offline, and, whatever you do, don't try to contact anyone after you've seen the contents of the chip. It would be a good idea to leave your comp system in stand-by mode for the rest of the day.

"When you've finished doing that, put the chip and this note in the container of fluid in the box and bury the whole works in a hole about a meter deep, at least a hundred meters south of your corral, and cover it well—please, be careful. It would be a good idea to use those heavy rubber gloves you keep in the kitchen. Put them on before you open the container and be sure you don't inhale any of the fumes. This is powerful and nasty stuff.

"Love you baby. Your mom says, hello. Hugs and kisses to the kids. "See you later, Dad..."

She set the note aside, dumped the contents of the envelope out on the table and sat there, wide-eyed for a moment. The envelope had been full of Wesblocs. She began counting the money. When she reached twenty thousand, she went, shaking, to the coffee maker and set it to extra strong, then returned to finish counting.

Fifty thousand blocs? That's enough to live on for two years—three, if we were frugal. Okay, Dad, what's this about?

With trembling fingers she disconnected the vid, com system and computer, then slipped the chip into the playback slot. After that, she went on uncertain legs to the kitchen counter and poured her coffee. Her father had always been a strange and secretive man, but she couldn't remember a time when he had acted like this. If he had something to tell her he would just call, and he didn't include envelopes filled with thousands of blocs or containers of acid to dispose of the evidence. Whatever this was, it was important. She sat there, pensively sipping at her coffee and staring at the stuff strewn before her on the table while she debated whether she would wait for Morgan to come home before she played the chip.

* * *

17 January 2054: 0930 MST

A tall man, wearing a black padded and heated snowsuit, stood in the dining room, turning a glass cup with a gold Navy emblem on it in his gloved hands. The coffee in it was a solid block of dark brown ice with a frosty white surface. He looked up at another man standing in the doorway and said, "This is just great...just great. Is there any way to know which way they went?"

"Not a chance. It's been snowing all night,

man. The ground around here has been frozen solid all week. The walls in the garage are showing no local signs of residual heat, so they've been out of here at least twelve hours, probably longer, unless they were running on electric when they left. If that were the case, they could have left as little as three hours before we got here. There's nothing showing on the ground, either. If you were to ask me, I'd say this guy knows what he's doing. No maps...no notes...nothing."

"Yeah, it sure looks that way, doesn't it? By the look of the coffee in this cup, they left closer to your first estimate. Get me a record on him." He threw the cup he was holding into the kitchen and it shattered against the ceramic tile floor, the coffee in it skittered to the far corner like a hockey puck.

"They're driving an old Hummer hybrid, so they couldn't have gone too far. Not in this weather, anyway. Get us an infrared scan of a five hundred klick block centered on this place and have them run radar, too. Infrared isn't going to show us much through a freezing overcast and light snowfall. Tell them we're interested in anything that shows up off the roads. And I mean, anything, moving or not. There are bound to be some breaks in the cloud cover somewhere."

He withdrew a map from his suit and spread it out on the table. "For such a crummy little state, they sure have a hell of a lot of roads and trails," he said to the empty room. "No way we can cover all of them. We should've thrown a net over this puke the first time around."

17 January 2054: 0935 MST

"Well, we're more than fifty klicks due east of Engle. Now we turn east. At this rate we should make it to Highway 54 and come out a little north of Tularosa in about an hour and a half. We'll be on real roads again," Wendell Stone said, staring at the GPS screen on the dash where a topographic map of the mountainous terrain surrounding them was displayed. "Pour me another coffee, Hon."

"How long before we get to Carlsbad, Dad?"

"We'll be coming out on the flats in a half hour and we should get to Dyllan's place no later than five. We'll have this thing hidden in his barn in fifteen minutes. That is, if they don't find us first."

"But you don't know Dyllan that well. What if he doesn't want us to stay with him? And I still don't understand what makes you think they're after us," Lolly Stone said.

"That's exactly why we're going there. Dyllan's will be one of the last on their list of places to look, if they find out about him, and I'm relying on that to give us the time we need to get ready. Maybe I know Dyllan better than you think, sweety. He'll let us stay, trust me. As far as how it is I know they're after us, all you have to do is remember what I did for twenty- five miserable years. I know how they work, and that visit of theirs served as a warning to me. Then that couple from Cal Western University came by and tied up the whole package nice and neat. For some reason, what Jerry reported to the Union is at the bottom of this—and I think I might know what that reason is. If I'm right, they can't afford to have any of us running around loose."

"And what if you're wrong?"

"If I'm wrong, and I'm willing to bet my last bloc that I'm not, we will have had a thrilling off-road ride through the mountains in a whiteout, and a nice visit with Dyllan and Carolyn. One of the great things about being retired is having the time to do fun stuff like this."

"Fun? You call this fun?"

"Sure. When was the last time you had a chance to drive blind and off-road in conditions even a jackrabbit is too smart to go out in?"

* * *

17 January 2054: 1045 MST

One of the men in the back seat leaned forward enough to get the attention of their leader, who was sitting in the front passenger seat.

"Yeah? What?"

"The info you wanted on our boy just came through."

"Well, who and what is he?"

"You're gonna love this. First, though, we're ISA agents, right?"

"Yeah, what of it?"

"We should have ready access to any damned thing we want, right?"

"Will you get to the point?"

54

"It took me more than an hour of arm twisting and threatening remarks to get this stuff, and I have a sneaking suspicion it's not everything there is—like they're holding back some things they'd rather we didn't know."

"The info, damn it."

"Our man, Stone, if that's really his name, has a dossier thicker than New York Metro air. He has more names and papers to back them up than most dictionaries have words—and his current history stops just ten years back. Nothing on him between forty-four and now."

"Will you, please, give me the bottom line?"

"All right. All right. Wendell Stone was a Navy Seal for twenty-five years. Oh, by the way, there's no name given for him during that time—just a code number. He was a forward ops guy, but not just any forward ops guy. Two years inside the Iran-Iraq Union; three years in China; four years in Siberia; four years as a roving operative in western Europe. He speaks nine languages and, according to the powers that be, is an organizational genius. He's on a first name basis with people in high places you and I will never see and in low places we don't want to see. He holds a Masters in mathematics and a PhD in physics. He's supposed to be retired, but from the detail they left out, he's probably still active in some way. Probably CIA or something worse. Shall I continue?"

"Not now. I'll look through the file when we get to the field office in El Paso. At least we know we're not going to find this bastard the normal way...even though he's lugging his family along.

Sure got lucky for our first assignment, didn't we?"

* * *

17 January 2054: 1220 MST

Curiosity grew all morning, and Roberta Hathaway couldn't stand it any longer. She reached out, hesitantly, for the playback button on the panel, then drew her hand away. Morgan needs to see it, too, she thought. If it were as important as her father made it appear in his note, she should wait for Morgan. But, on the other hand, he wanted all the evidence destroyed and their comp not offline too long. That meant, to her, that time might be as important as content and more important than family diplomacy. She had just put the kids down for their nap, so there was no better time. She reached out again, but this time she punched the button and the screen lit up with the image of her father, sitting in his den.

"Hi, Bobby. I know this all looks pretty weird to you, but it's really, really important. Life and death important. I'm not going to waste any time here, so listen carefully and use your magnificent memory to make certain you don't forget anything.

"If he's not there right now, get across to Morgan that what I'm telling you is going to affect your future—all our futures—the whole world's future. The reason I've chosen to make contact this way is because there is no way for me to know if they have our system or yours tapped, but I don't think there's much doubt about it. What I want you

56

to do is, pack up the kids and head for a little town in southeastern New Mexico named Jal. It's about fifty kilometers south of Hobbs, just off State Highway 18. Uncle Dan owns some property and a couple of houses there. You are going to stay in one of them until we come to pick you up. That won't be any longer than three weeks from now. More than likely, sooner.

"Dan will meet you at a restaurant in Jal—the Tortilla Flats Fiesta. There aren't many restaurants there so I know you won't have any trouble finding it. Do what he tells you, Bobby—and don't argue. We can't afford to make any mistakes, or we're all in deep stinko.

"Take all—all of your credit cards and toss them in the container I sent, along with this chip and my note. Don't keep anything. Don't withdraw any money you have in the bank. Just use what you found in the envelope. Before you leave the house, take the system off stand-by and don't say anything after you've done it. Just go out the door and lock it.

Don't take any clothes except whatever you choose to wear for the trip. Dan will have what you need.

"Morgan, before you pack everyone in the car, disconnect the com system and the emergency locator, then get in and go. And drive carefully. No tickets or we're out of luck. By the time you're in the car, the data from the courier will be on the general grid, and they'll be aware I contacted you. I'm not going to try to explain all of this right now, but something is going to happen that will change everything. Everything. Now, get going and don't forget what I've told you.

"We love you and we'll be seeing you soon."

Her father was always joke-ready, and prone to make light of anything and everything. She had never seen him look and sound so serious, so somber. She played the chip through twice more, made sure it had wiped, then went to the kitchen to get her gloves and the small garden spade she kept under the sink.

Chapter 3

18 January 2054: 0720 MST

The two children were sleeping soundly in the back seat when they pulled into the little town of Jal. It had been a harrowing and tiring trip, in spite of the long stretch of auto-drive on the main highways, when they were both able to get a few hours of sleep. Near blizzard conditions were behind them by no more than the half hour drive down from Hobbs. A mix of ice and snow was still falling lightly, but being whipped around by a strong wind. Roberta Hathaway was painfully aware of the prolonged silence between them. She could feel Morgan's anger and frustration through the entire trip and she was about to say something to break the silence, but Morgan did it first.

"All I can say is, this had better be one hell of a story with a mountain of importance to back it up. I just walked out on a good job with a future in it—something you don't stumble into every day in these times of outsourcing to every other piddling third world country on the globe, huh? He didn't even give you a tiny clue as to what this is about.?"

"No, but he wouldn't have gone to all the trouble of getting a private courier to carry the package and he wouldn't have sent such a huge bundle of cash without good reason. You know my dad."

"Yeah, and that's the only reason we're here, but I have to tell you, I'm just a little more than torqued by all of this."

"I know. I know, but I'm sure he has—oh, there it is, up there on the right, Tortilla Flats Fiesta. Anyway, we'll know more in a few minutes. He's sure to have told Uncle Dan something."

The parking lot was empty except for two older compacts parked out front and a beat up and battered, thirty-year old four-by-four pick-up truck off to one side. Morgan slipped their car into the charging line and linked up. They left the children sleeping in the car and made a dash through the driving sleet and snow to the restaurant.

Inside, there was no sign of her uncle, so they grabbed a table by the window where they could keep a watch on the car, just in case the children awakened while they were eating.

"You told me he said that Dan would be waiting for us."

"He did, but it's pretty early and we don't know—"

"Well, there you are," a gruff voice said from the pass-through window to the kitchen. "Amy, get in here and take over the kitchen for me. What would you kids like—besides coffee? And where the hell are my little ones?"

The owner of the voice stepped out of the kitchen, threw a grease stained apron in a basket by the door, and approached the table where Roberta and Morgan Hathaway sat. Daniel Klein was a big man in all respects and a three-day growth of blacker than coal beard shadowed his face. His long, black hair, streaked with hints of gray, was tied back tightly in a ponytail. His left arm bore a tattoo of a serpent that began at his wrist and coiled

60

up around his arm until its head disappeared under the sleeve of his black tee shirt. On the front of his shirt were the words, "SUBMIT OR DIE." He didn't look anything at all like his brother.

Roberta jumped up from the table and threw her arms around him.

He responded in kind, thrust out a huge hand to Morgan, then took a seat at the table.

"You guys have come a long way in the dark— I mean, the not knowing anything kind of dark. You'd better sit down because this is heavy shit. The guv's going to be after all of us and that means I have to leave, too."

"What? Why?" Morgan Hathaway asked.

"Well, according to what Em said, we're in for a hell of a beating in a few years. Comets are coming, lots of'em. He said the first ones that are going to hit—and one of'em's a big sucker—will be here in the last part of June in sixty-one, probably on the twenty-fifth. And he said the guv's got a program up and running to keep anything from getting out to the public about it. That's why we have to vanish. He said they would use the families of those who are in the know to keep them in line— that's us. Frankly, I don't much give a damn about me, being alone like I am since Angela died, except I don't go for the idea of being locked up, and I sure as hell don't like the idea of being thrown in the cooler just because my kid brother's a smart- ass college grad, you know?"

"That's...that's more than seven years from now," Morgan Hathaway protested. "Why do we have to run now?"

61

"I just told you why. They'll be out gathering up families because they can't be sure what they might know or who they might talk to. Because they're related to these people, people like Em and Sandy. Because they can use us to keep them from saying anything to anyone else...and because they're a bunch of paranoid—"

"Okay. I get the idea. So, what are we supposed to do?"

"Well, originally, Em said we could spend a couple of weeks just hiding out here. He changed his mind on that and said we need to go now—today."

"Where?" Roberta asked.

"Carlsbad. We're all going to Carlsbad. Don't ask me why, because I don't know. Em didn't say. All he said was for us to get there ASAP and that they'd meet us at the Carlsbad Inn tomorrow morning about nine. We'll leave your car here and Amy will do what needs to be done. Just leave the key on the table, you won't be needing it any more. Morgan, you know how to drive that old pick-up out there?"

"Um, yeah. That's the first kind of vehicle I learned to drive. Dad had a couple of them on the ranch in Montana and we used them all the time...until gas went over seven blocs a gallon, anyway."

"That one's been converted to hydrogen, so we don't have that problem. Driving it is the same as a gas rig, though. We'll make a quick run out to the house and clean out the bed of the truck. I've got a load of crap to put in it, then we go," Daniel Klein said. "Amy, it's all yours, babe. You know what to do with the houses and the car. I suggest you close up now and get started on that, before it gets too late."

"What? No kiss good-bye, or nothing, Mike?" Amy called out from the kitchen.

"Mike?" Roberta Hathaway said. "Tell you about that, later."

* * *

18 January 2054: 0745 MST

The ISA field office in El Paso was filled with people moving quickly from one cubicle to another, all of them wearing serious purpose in their expressions. Marvin Scolini barged into the director's office unannounced, a stack of data chips in one hand. He threw the chips onto the desktop in front of the director and scowled. "This one got away from us," Scolini said, literally spitting out the words.

"Calm down, and let's try this again. Who got away from us?"

"Wendell Stone. Name ring any bells for you?"

"No. Should it?"

"You damn right it should. This one's dangerous, I mean really dangerous, and I want to know why we didn't have all the information that's on those chips in our database before we went looking for him. I also want to know why those chips don't have all there is to know about this guy. Why are we being stonewalled by the same

63

government that set up this program in the first place?"

"They wouldn't stonewall us—Scolini, is it?"

"That's right."

"Well, Scolini, I'm sure there must be a reasonable explanation...if there is missing information in our database. Why don't you go out and get a coffee or something, while I look into it. I'll give you a call when I know more, all right?"

Scolini left the office, his face as red as the early morning, smoke-filled sky brought on by illegal trash fires and the burning of old tires on the other side of the river. Forty years since the signing of the new pact between the two cities and no one had figured out a way to enforce it yet. He grabbed his second in command and dragged him out of the building.

"Where are we going?"

"We're going to sit in a nice, warm restaurant, away from all this political shitical, and suck on some coffee while our infinitely wise Director of Operations goes through the info you got on Stone. Then, he said, if we are really missing data on him, he'll check out how come we don't have it and give me a call. Can you beat that? Genuine bureaucratic efficiency. What would you like to bet he doesn't find anything more than we did?"

"No bet. They'll probably stiff him like they did us. My money's still on that guy not being fully retired, like he's still working on something they want to keep covered up. I can't think of any other reason for them not wanting to give us what we need."

18 January 2054: 0950 EST

"Aw, come on, Elaine. There have been five heavy launches from the Cape in the last five days, and not a single one announced in advance—not one word about them. You know as well as I do that it takes months of prep to get even one of those things off the ground. The whole Cape is now off limits to anyone. I hear they've also put a full court press on getting the space elevator in operation ahead of their own schedule. That's a government project, and if they manage to beat the schedule it'll be the miracle of the century that you'd think they'd want to advertise. You don't call that some kind of suspicious?"

"Yes, Mel, I call that curious activity. I also call it the government's business. The fact that they're not handing out brochures to the press and inviting us in for photo ops is proof of that."

"Do you mind if I spend a little of my time trying to find out what's going on?"

"Hell no, I don't mind—as long as it's your time we're talking about, not mine—and I get an exclusive on whatever you find out—if it's juicy.

That is, as long as you meet your deadlines and keep up your usual high level of mediocre reporting, whatever else you do is up to you. If the stuff from the Cape's not hot, screw it. Oh, don't forget to hustle your little tush out to Epcot to cover the opening of Virtual Mars next week. Now, get out of my office."

Mellisa Landers gathered up her photos of the unannounced launches from Elaine's desk, stuffed them back into the folder, and left. She didn't stop by her desk on the way out, either. She needed fresh air and she needed to be as far away from the office as she could get before she succumbed to her desire to go back in and bite that acrimonious bitch's head off.

Five heavy launches in as many days was more than "curious activity".

Those giant boosters cost gigablocs to send up and they took time to get ready, so they weren't doing it for the excitement or the fireworks. There was a reason and she was going to find out what it was. After three blocks of brisk walking, she turned in to Terrington's Tampa to get something to eat. She wasn't hungry, but she had shifted into attack reporter mode and needed to think. Food sitting in front of her, eaten or not, served as the catalyst for that process.

She took a table by the western windows with a view of the beach and the soft green waters of the Gulf of Mexico to sooth her nerves and aid her concentration. By the time her order arrived, she had determined there was enough in the bank, plus what she could get from a mortgage on the house to go independent for at least four years without starving. She also knew she was not going to be able to approach this thing directly. They had sealed off the Cape. They had made no mention of what was happening in any venue, and the OPI wasn't answering any calls. The NASA field office in

Jacksonville was open to calls but everyone she wanted to talk to had conveniently just stepped out for lunch, been called to a meeting, or were off on extended vacations. Conclusion? They didn't want anyone to know anything about their activities out at the Cape and they hadn't come up with a cover story to feed the avidly curious—yet.

On a napkin she compiled a list of people who might be in a position to help her in her quest and set up a logical order to make contact with as many as she could in as short a time as possible. Then she began picking at her food while she thought through the whole thing again.

* * *

18 January 2054: 1025 EST

Albert Zweig opened the door just enough to see who was outside.

His only visible eye through the crack he'd allowed the door to make squinted at the brightness.

"Mel?"

"Yep, it's your favorite, pesky little investigative reporter. Can I come in?"

Zweig slipped out the door, and led her away from his apartment as if she was the second girlfriend who had shown up at a bad time. "What the hell is this, Al?"

"Just shut up and keep walking. We're going to the bar on the corner.

We'll talk when we get there. Now is not the time. They're around and they're probably listening."

She had known Albert Zweig for more than ten years and he had never acted like this, and he never went to bars. She didn't say anything—but she was certainly going to when they got to the bar. When they reached the East End Bar and Grill on the corner, Zweig shoved her through the classic, saloon-style doors, latched on to her arm again and half dragged her to a dark, corner table, even though the place was vacant, except for the bartender who was busily toweling a row of glasses into spotless brilliance.

"Have you talked to anyone else, Mel?" he demanded, his voice low and strained.

"I talk to lots of people every day. That's what I do for a living.

What's happening with the megalaunches and what the hell are you so afraid of, Al?"

"Have you talked to anyone else associated with NASA or the space program in general in the last week, Mel? It's important."

"Well, yes. I've called several NASA offices—got nowhere—and I've tried to get through to the Cape and the OPI line with the same results.

Why?"

"I was afraid of that. You and your prying nose. You noticed the launches while you were out there last week, no doubt, and your famous curiosity overrode your sensible side, as always. They'll probably be looking for you now, and I suggest you find yourself a deep hole and hide in it for a few years. I mean it, Mel."

"What...what are you talking about."

"I'm not going to give you any details, Mel, but you're going to be swimming in a pile of crap up to your eyeballs if they find out you've been calling around. Oh, what the hell am I saying? They probably already know. Damn it, Mel, just take whatever you have, convert it to cash as fast as you can, and get the hell out of Dodge. Make sure you have a believable story for why you're leaving, and go any place where no one knows you—don't use your car to do it, either. Don't use any form of transportation that requires ID. And stay the hell away from people like me. It's for your own good. And the next time you see someone carrying a sign that says, 'The End is Coming', don't laugh." He giggled an insane little laugh like a small child who has gotten away with something horrid, and stood up from the table. Without so much as a 'nice to have seen you, Mel', Albert Zweig sprinted to the door, looked up and down the street as if he were an amateur crook dodging the law, then ran off toward his apartment. Mellisa Landers sat in silent stupor for a few minutes while she tried to piece together the meaning behind Zweig's weird behavior.

The bartender's voice drifted through her mental haze and shocked her back into the world of the present. "Excuse me, ma'am. You want a sandwich or something? I can't serve anything alcoholic until after twelve."

* * *

18 January 2054: 0830 MST

69

Marvin Scolini looked up from his third cup of watered down fast-food- restaurant coffee and winked at his second in command, Allen Worth, then pulled the boom mic down from his head and said, "Scolini here." He sat listening to the voice in his earpiece, then said, "Yes, sir, will do."

"Will do what?" Worth said.

Scolini broke into a roar of laughter that brought the pair the attention of several early morning burger addicts.

"What? What's so damned funny?"

"Our illustrious leader is royally pissed, man. I mean steaming, man. Everything he tried failed. We don't get anything more on Stone than what we already know. All he could say was that Stone is one of our hard cases. Mr. Your Highness, Director of Operations, says we are to find this guy, and find him quick. He wants this bastard at any cost, and he said that the sooner we find him, the better. He's even being generous and assigning two of those investigator types to our team to aid us in our search. That means we're going to be dragging around the extra weight of two badly dressed guys who wear sunglasses at midnight. What the hell does he think we are, magicians or something?"

Worth squirmed in the plastic seat and said, "You know, I've been thinking, Marv. We've been trained to do this job, right?"

"Yeah?"

"And the investigation squads give us a list of people to bring in, right? That list includes wives, kids—the whole damned family."

"Yeah. So, what?"

70

"So, there's something missing from the picture that's starting to bother me one hell of a lot."

"Okay, Allen, let's hear it."

"We don't have the slightest idea of why we're going out there to bring them in, other than that they're supposed to be a threat to internal security. I mean, what did they do? How are they a threat? Are they terrorists, or people with ties to terrorist groups? What? At least the cops know that much before they go nabbing people off the street. We...we don't know squat."

"You like the size of your monthly credit allotment, Allen?"

"Yeah, sure."

"So, what's to know? We just do our job and draw our pay. End of story, right?"

Chapter 4

Emery Klein was never one for making a lot of small talk. After a brief reunion, and the two children went out to the enclosed play area next to the Carlsbad Inn's restaurant, he got down to the business of letting everyone in on what they were facing.

"Now, listen," he said. "What this is about is the coming end of the world as we know it, and there is nothing we can do to prevent it. Wipe the smirk off your face, Morgan, this is as serious as it gets, and no amount of denial will make it go away. By my last crude calculations, which I did late yesterday afternoon, we are going to be hit by no less than ten large comets between June and December of 2061. Only a small number of them are big enough to cause worldwide problems by themselves, but collectively they will change everything—everywhere—forever.

"Just two or three of those rocks would do the job, but we know there are a lot more of them than that. How many more, we can't say. There may be hundreds, perhaps thousands that could hit us over the years after sixty-one. It won't be just the impacts that do the damage and raise all the dust, either. The earth itself is going to aid in that by becoming volcanically and seismically more active than it has been since the period of heavy bombardment during the formation of the early solar system."

72

"What?" Morgan Hathaway said. "How can that be?"

"Something occurred, probably several millions of years ago, that disturbed the paths of the icy bodies way outside the orbit of Echo," Sandra Klein said. "We didn't notice anything odd in the orbits of the objects out there that we were able to see because they were much too massive and their orbits had stabilized aeons before we humans ever thought about anything more than filling our bellies and not being eaten by predators. The smaller ones, the ones easiest to move and the stuff we couldn't see, went unnoticed, until this month when the first groups of them were spotted by amateur comet hunters."

"And," her husband continued, "the result of all those impacts will be a winter that will last at least a hundred years, maybe a lot longer. Deadly radiation will follow when the cloud of dust encircling the planet has dissipated because the ozone will have been seriously depleted. That, coupled with acid rains and severe storms, the likes of which no one has ever seen, will be generated in the atmosphere on a global scale. Human survival will depend on knowledge and advanced planning. Our only hope is to set up our own colony in a safe place and wait however long it takes for things to settle."

"Holy shit. Is this for real?" Morgan Hathaway said, having lost all interest in his breakfast. The smirk had also disappeared.

"No doubt about it," Emery Klein said. "Now, the reason for all this secrecy. The governments of the world, not just ours, have a program to save an elite group, probably numbering in the thousands, from the disaster. When the conditions permit, their descendants will emerge and begin the rebuilding process. None of us, I'm sure, are included on their lists. But it gets worse. In order to keep the population of the planet from going into a state of panic too soon, they have also instituted programs to keep knowledge of the coming disaster from getting out and, at the moment, that is our number one problem."

"I guess that means they're going to throw anyone who knows anything in jail?" Roberta Hathaway said.

"Not exactly," her mother said. "There are too many of us and not enough jails to go around. Your dad and I believe that they have set up camps to house the dangerous people, us, until the last minute—until it's too late...and all of the chosen ones are tucked safely away somewhere."

"But that's...mass murder," Roberta Hathaway protested.

"It's not exactly murder, Bobby, but that's the only thing we can come up with that seems to make any sense. They may even be willing to kill some—a lot of people outright, if they think it's necessary, and that would be murder of a sort," her father continued. "That's the reason we're all here. I intend for us to survive—whatever happens—and I mean for us to remain free while we prepare for what's coming. Our lives depend on it.

Your mother and I want to see our grandchildren grow up, and not behind the fences of some concentration camp run by a latter day gang of black- suited SS brutes."

"Just us?"

"No, baby. Others will surely come to the same conclusions that your mom and I did, and a lot of them will think of this place, too. Probably too many, then we'll be faced with the same kind of decisions the government is having to make now. A kind of predictable irony that we'll have to accept...whether we like it or not. We are going to need a ton of help to do what we will have to do, and that means we'll have to recruit a bunch of people who can be trusted. That's where Dan comes in."

"Aha! So that's it," Daniel said, wearing a knowing grin. "Okay, Uncle Dan," Morgan Hathaway said. "What's it?"

"The caverns, dummy," Daniel retorted. "He wants to use them for protection from whatever the hell he thinks is going to happen here."

* * *

19 January 2054: 1040 MST

When she stepped off the bus in El Paso, she was hit square in the face—and other places—with an unexpected, cruel reality. It was bone jarring cold and her attire didn't do her any favors. Her jeans were barely heavy enough, but her thin blouse and no bras, fine for the Tampa weather, definitely didn't make it. For some reason she had thought it would be warm in the southwestern desert, but she disembarked into a snow and ice flurry.

She made a mad dash for the depot doors while goose bumps sprang up all over her body. On the way she spotted three men in black uniforms, uniforms she didn't recognize, brandishing nasty-looking weapons. The men watched people getting off the bus with the frightening intensity of starving foxes searching for a way into the henhouse. Once inside, she encountered a group of young people dressed in cotton togas that swept the floor. They all chanted a monotone mantra, rattled tambourines, and thumped on small drums with little sticks. One of them carried a placard tacked to a piece of wood that read, "Repent, for the END is near."

'...don't laugh,' Zweig had said. Mellisa Landers didn't laugh, just ducked under the edge of the bobbing sign and headed for the coffee shop, her back pack and purse hanging from one hand and a large briefcase from the other—all of them filled with blocs. Her nipples rubbed against the coarse material of her blouse, and hurt like hell.

The quality of people who inhabited bus stations, particularly in cold weather, hadn't improved since she was a little girl and traveled with her mother from LA Metroplex to Tampa. They were dirt poor then, and her father had just died in the war that forced a loose and unstable Iran-Iraq Union into being—hammered into place like the proverbial square peg in a round hole. She had been afraid of the depot denizens then, and it was worse now, what with a couple hundred thousand blocs in her possession. She was glad she had chosen not to wear any jewelry or clothes that would draw attention to her, except for that damned loose-knit, almost see through blouse with her nipples standing erect.

She slipped her back pack over her shoulders and got into line at the cafeteria-style counter. She needed coffee and something—anything—to eat. She had chosen to come on a real express bus that made only one stop in the whole trip and neglected to bring anything to drink or munch on.

Stupid move for a brilliant, ace reporter, she thought. The only available table was a mushroom-looking thing with a stained, crumb-and-other-stuff covered yellow top on a dingy white base. The chair beside it was light blue plastic, deeply discolored from who-knew-what, and cracked in several places. She put her briefcase and handbag in the seat, swept the crumbs off the table, and set a small, purple tray down in the cleanest spot she could find.

The interior decorator of this dump had to have been color blind, or on drugs.

Inside a fold-up plastic box she found a rather homogeneous looking yellow slab that the menu declared to be scrambled eggs. The yellow plank was trying to hide beneath a paper thin patty of crisp fried sausage.

Alongside rested a dollop of what they said were supposed to be hash-brown potatoes. A white plastic fork-cum-spoon-cum-knife in a clear plastic bag lay tucked under the potatoes. Sprinkled over the top of the whole mess were several tear-open packets of ketchup and something called South of the Border Fire. She didn't toy with her food this time, but dove in and devoured the entire order, including the South of the Border Fire, in something less that three minutes.

For the next fifteen minutes she sat and sipped at her coffee, thinking about where she was and what she needed to do next. Hiding from something unknown, hiding from anything really, was new to her. She was accustomed to confronting anything on a face-to-face basis, but Zweig scared the hell out of her with his obvious and emotion-filled concern over something he had been unwilling to talk about. A few blocks south of her lay the border. Mexico?

No—that's too complicated, and I could wind up trapped down there, separated from my money with no way out.

"...find yourself a deep hole and hide in it for a few years." Maybe he wasn't speaking figuratively. Maybe he really meant for her to find a hole. What hole? Thoughts were coming to her. Crazy thoughts. Find a hole. Where?

She went to the store next to the cafeteria and bought a long, down- filled jacket with a padded hood, yanked all the tags off it and put it on, then she went to the ticket counter and purchased a one-way ticket to Carlsbad, New Mexico.

* * *

19 January 2054: 0945 PST

"I really need to see them, ma'am. Did they leave any messages for anyone that might indicate where they have gone or when they will return?"

"No. As I said before, the university is closed today, as far as scheduled class activities are

78

concerned. MLK day, you know, but we did have a meeting arranged that called for all department heads to be here this morning at 8:30. It was a rather poor turnout, I'll tell you. I imagine that was because they all wanted their long weekend and either couldn't get back or conveniently forgot. Whatever the reason, neither of the Kleins showed up, either. I'm sure they'll all be here tomorrow, or I can have the secretary call their home before she leaves for the day, if you would like."

"No. No thank you, ma'am. That won't be necessary, but thank you very much for your offer. We'll just go back out there and see if they've come home yet. Thanks, again."

Outside, the man who had been speaking to the Dean turned to his associate. "Well, I think your suspicion of the Kleins was right, Norman. Put a call in to round up the whole family. I'm going across the street to the bookstore—see if either of them bought any books recently that might give us a clue about what they might be up to."

"Bookstore's closed."

"Yeah, so it is. MLK day. Well, we'll just have to open it, won't we?"

* * *

19 January 2054: 1100 MST

"Scolini, what are you doing in here? I thought I told you to get Stone for me. From what I can see, he's not in my office or the holding cell—and I don't see any body bags in the hall."

79

"No, sir. We don't have him yet...but we will. I just thought I'd give you something else to worry about."

"I'm worried up to my nostrils already. Now what?"

"Some of our own people are asking questions. Uncomfortable questions, sir."

"Oh? Who's doing the asking?"

"My second, for one. And if he's asking, it's damned certain others are, too."

"You mean, Worth? What kind of questions is he asking?"

"Why we're after these people. He wants to know what they've done."

"What about you, Scolini? Do you wonder why we're doing this?"

"Me? I know why I'm doing it, and I don't give a rat's ass what they've done. I do my job. And when I get my orders, I follow them. As long as the blocs keep getting credited to my account, I'm a happy trooper. I just thought you'd like to know so you could start keeping an eye on our own."

"I appreciate that, Scolini. Tell Worth I'd like to see him—now. While I take care of that, you can pick his replacement from the pool. Now, get out of here and bring me Stone and family."

"Does it matter to you how I bring them in?"

"Not even a little bit. If you need to, you can bring them in small pieces, for all I care. Just get Stone, and that kid of his—and no, I don't care about him, either. Whatever you need to do, just get them."

In the outer office there were several ISA

Enforcement Agents waiting to talk to the Sector Chief. Scolini motioned to Allen Worth, who was standing in a corner of the waiting area with a small group of other agents. Probably talking about things that don't concern them, Scolini thought.

"Hey, Allen. The boss wants to see you...now." Worth pointed a finger at himself and gave a questioning shrug. "Yeah, you. You are Enforcement Agent Allen Worth, aren't you?"

"What does he want with me?"

"Don't have the foggiest. He just said he wants to see you now.

Probably going to give you a raise or a promotion, or something," Scolini said, accompanying the statement with a wicked laugh.

* * *

19 January 2054: 1155 MST

"Okay, Wendell, let's have it. What the hell are you doing out here? From the stuff I can tell is hiding under the tarp on that trailer of yours, you're not here to pay me a friendly visit—and you're not here for just a few days of vacation, either."

"Right on both counts. Let's go out to the barn and you can help me offload the nukes and put them in your safe room, all right?"

The two of them walked out toward the barn, a large, dilapidated rusted steel structure about a hundred meters west of Dyllan Drake's house, neither of them talking on the way. The early morning sprinkling of light snow had finally stopped and the sun was showing through the thin overcast. When they reached the doors, Dyllan sent the signal that activated them. The doors opened on a modern building that had been built a meter inside the deliberately distressed outer shell. Once inside, with the doors closed, they resumed their conversation.

"Dyllan, do you remember the camp we liberated in Iran?"

"Oh, yeah—who could forget? Poor slobs. Combatants or not, no one deserves to be treated like that. What's that have to do with you being here, and why the nuke cells and satellite transmitter, old buddy?"

"I'm not sure of this yet, but I have reason to believe our own government is doing something like that here—totally different reason, of course—and it's probably happening around the world. Camps going up all over. The conditions are probably better in some places than in others, but they're still concentration camps, whichever way you slice it, and, like you, I need to vanish for a time."

"What the hell for?"

"Because Jerry and I have some information that they want to keep from getting out to the public, and I'm damned certain, if they find us, we'll wind up in one of their camps—or dead—Lolly, too."

Wendell Stone went on to explain everything that had happened after that night in his son's observatory and Dyllan Drake listened intently. When Wendell finished, Drake and he went out to the Hummer parked next to the doors and began untying the lashings holding the tarp to the trailer.

"We had best get these nukes below," Dyllan said. "The shielding on this building is good, but these babies will show a trace fingerprint, even through the shielding, that satellites can pick up if they're looking for it. So, why here, and why me?"

"A lot of reasons. First, your place is close to the caverns. We're going to need them if we want to survive what's coming. Second, no one knows where you are and more than likely won't know any time soon. My big mistake was in not disappearing, too, when I had the chance. But, then, I didn't have the incentive you did, and I mistakenly thought I had left most of that crap behind me. Lack of foresight, I guess. Third, you're the best hacker that ever walked on this planet, and I'm going to need your talent to search the grid for information."

"You could do that—"

"Not the way you can. We need to get into some top level government systems. You can climb into the president's panties and get out without her ever knowing you were there, and that's what we need to do now. I want to find out what the ISA is, how it's structured, where its main points of operation are, and the names of the people who are in charge. If possible, I'd also like to dig up the locations of their camps, if that's what they're doing with the people they're hunting. Then, I need info on what it is they intend to do and how they plan to go about doing it, although I think I can guess that part of it."

"That's a tall order, Wendell."

"Yeah, I know. Think you can do it?"

"Can I do it? Can I do it? Have you ever known me to back down from a challenge like that? When I get done, if they find out I was there at all, they'll think it was an inside job and start lopping off heads in their own computer sections. According to what you've said, this thing probably does go all the way to the top and I may have to wander around in the president's trousers—uh, skirt—for awhile, too. When do you want me to start?"

"We don't need to rush it, and it's probably best if we don't. I'd say we can wait a couple of days until their level of confidence has exceeded their meager intelligence. Right now, as nervous as they probably are about a program this big, they're going to be watching things pretty close."

"Yeah, you're more than likely right about that. So, what's with the nukes? And four of them, at that."

"If what I think is going to happen does, we're going to need as much power as we can get for a long time. These little honeys will give us most of what we'll need for at least a hundred years. We're also going to have to put some stuff together while we're waiting to make sure we survive what's going to come after it begins."

"You think we're going to get hit by what you saw, right?"

"Not necessarily by what we saw but, according to what those folks from the university said, we're going to get clobbered by a lot of stuff and we don't have too long to fool around before it starts. A big storm's coming, Dyllan—a big storm."

***

Mellisa Landers got off the bus in the old city center of Carlsbad and shivered, not from the cold but because of the bleak surroundings. At least there were none of those imposing black uniforms standing around with guns. The small depot was almost empty, run down, and in need of paint; its brick walls as drab as the overcast, no contrast sky. Everywhere she looked there were vacant store fronts, broken windows gaping. A ghost town, she thought.

Where is everybody?

She weaved her way through the cars that were leaving the depot, new arrivals or returnees squashed into the tiny volume afforded by electric bubble commuters with all their baggage in their laps that couldn't be strapped down on top. All of them seemed to be in a hurry to leave this part of the city. She wondered where they were going, then went inside to buy a cup of coffee from an ancient machine. It was severely dented in the sides from the angry kicks administered by disgruntled customers who thought they had been cheated out of a bloc for a cup of dirty water. The machine stood alone, its once brightly colored plastic front missing, in a dingy corner where the cafeteria used to be, the skeleton of its counter not quite totally dismantled. She took the paper cup of tepid fluid and went to the ticket window for directions to the

85

closest motel. She needed a shower and a place to lie down—flat, for a change. An old man limped to the window as she approached. He was wearing a toothless, crooked smile smeared across his craggy, cracked face, his thumbs hooked behind broad suspenders.

"How can I help you today, missy?"

"Well, first of all, what happened here? I thought Carlsbad was a medium sized town."

"Yep. 'Twas until the automated bypassed us a few klicks east of here. Everythin' and everybody, them who could afford to, moved out there to the new highway and left us to rot. Ain't hardly nothin' here any more—nothin' that works worth a damn, anyway. I guess that includes me, huh? I heard they was gonna move the station out there, too, and I'll be outa work—just like that. What else can I do for you?"

"Is there a motel near here where I can get a room?"

"Yes'm. 'Bout five blocks north. Hope you don't mind sharin' the room."

"Sharing the room?"

"Yes'm. With the scorpions and cockroaches, that is. Um...that there was just a little spoof, missy. The straight dope is, the place is pretty clean—even close to modern, 'cept they're not linked to the grid no more.

Hardly nothin' out here is. If you want, you can call'em from here and they'll have your room ready for you when you get there. Want me to get a cab for you?"

"You still have cabs here?"

86

"Nope. Not here. They come out from the new city, but they do come over here."

"No. No thanks. I think I'd like to walk. I have some thinking to do."

"Suit yourself, missy—but it's kinda chilly out there, ain't it?"

Chapter 5

"Get anything yet?"

"Uh-huh. Their system is encrypted several different ways from Sunday, and at a bunch of levels, but I got through. It was obvious they didn't want anyone in there, though."

"Well?"

"Okay, Wendell. Okay. I managed to get in last night—2300 hours, their time. They're going to wonder why anyone in their building was traipsing around in their chip garden so late on a Sunday night, but they'll have to figure that out on their own, right? Anyway, I stayed in there as long as I dared and pulled out as much as I could. What I got jibes pretty well with what you thought was on their imaginary minds—but a whole lot worse than even you could have dreamed up."

"Did you keep the link?"

"Did I keep the link? What kind of a question is that? Did I keep the link? I'm the king of hackerdom, man. You keep asking me dumb questions like that and I'll send you packing."

"Well?"

"I can get in now whenever I want, but I think it would be a good idea not to do that for a few days—give them the time they need to write off what happened last night as a glitch in their system. I think it'll be safe to go back in sometime early next Sunday morning—we should be able to hang around all day. That'll get us everything we need, then I'll scramble their system for them so bad that they won't be able to find the date and time for a month."

"Wait a whole week?"

"Who's the hacker here?"

"Right. Okay, what did we get?"

"Well, for starters, we got some names, including the head men in the US, Germany, and Russia—and a few other places less civilized. More stars, braid and brass than a high school marching band. We have the operating regions here in the States, what they're calling 'Sectors', the number of camps allotted to each Sector, and the people in charge of all the Sectors.

When we go back in, I think we'll be able to get the locations of all the camps and nail down their communications frequencies, too. That should come in handy, don't you think? We are now privy to where the ISA came from and what their purpose is, too. I don't mind telling you, this is pretty scary stuff, man."

"Yeah, I thought it would be. Let's start organizing what we have in some reasonable order so we can come up with a tentative plan. I hate not knowing exactly what I'm facing and how I'm going to face it. Who's the head man for this program?"

"This Project Lazarus of theirs is sealed up tighter than the Manhattan Project was, and the guy in charge is a two star Army guy named Abram Walter Stoker. Ever heard of him?"

"No. They probably promoted him up from some little desk job at the Pentagon so they could hang their Lazarus anchor around his neck. He'll be in command of the project, but he'll also be their fall guy if it comes apart and the public gets their hands on it before they've done what they want to do. Typical. What about this ISA outfit?"

"Shit...shades of the Gestapo, the SS and the KGB all rolled into one nasty little ball, and their mandate comes directly from the top by presidential order. They have what amounts to carte blanche with this Lazarus thing...including the license to kill. They can pick up anyone they want, whenever they want, and do whatever they want. Looks to me like we need to dig in and stay out of sight. You know, hang tight."

"You can do whatever you think is necessary, I'm going to stay out here and break this whole thing apart. Whatever it takes, I'm going to see to it that Lazarus goes all the way to the grave this time, and doesn't have a chance to rise again."

And how, Mr. Superdupe Stone, do you propose to do that?"

"As soon as we have enough information and evidence, we go public via the news vid and pads. Let the world know what's going on and who's giving them the royal shaft."

"Yeah? How?"

"Dyllan, didn't you say you were the king of hackerdom?"

* * *

26 January 2054: 0900 MST

90

The cab pulled into the parking lot of the Carlsbad Pavilion Mall off the main automated where it turned east for Hobbs and larger cities on the eastern side of the state line.

"Here you go, lady," the driver said. "Over there on the right is the main entrance to the mall and the shuttle for the caverns loads right here where we're sitting. Don't forget, though, they don't get much traffic in the winter any more, not since the main entrance was shut down for repair, so you'll have plenty of time to get out here. It won't leave until ten-thirty or a little later. Whenever they have enough people to make the trip worth the trouble."

Landers thanked him for his help and paid what she felt was an exorbitant sixty blocs for a fifteen kilometer trip, plus an unearned tip, then strode off for the mall entrance. Being cooped up in her little room since she arrived in Carlsbad, venturing out only for an occasional walk to get the cobwebs out of her head and for meals proved too much for her. There was a great little café serving the most scrumptious of Mexican cuisine that opened early and closed late just two blocks north of the motel, and the Carlsbad Inn was a couple of blocks west when she wanted the meat, potatoes, and salad bar treatment, but that was it, and she wondered how they could stay in business.

Wearing the same clothes for over a week, washing them in the evenings and throwing them over the shower curtain bar to dry at night was getting on her nerves, too. She felt grungy, even though her clothes were clean. She entered the mall with nothing more on her mind than to expand her wardrobe and surround herself with people.

She wasn't paying any attention to the world around her. Her mind was focused on what Zweig told her back in Tampa and on her way out of the first store she visited, she ran headlong into a tiny, fragile-looking woman. The force of their meeting knocked the smaller woman down. The contents of the bags and boxes she was carrying scattered all over the floor.

"Oh, I'm so sorry," Landers said as she reached down to help the woman get back on her feet. "Are you all right?"

"Yes. Yes, I'm fine," the woman said, accepting Landers' hand. The two of them gathered up all the stuff from the floor, refilling bags and boxes as they went.

"I'm really sorry," Landers reiterated. "Let me treat you to a coffee, maybe a late breakfast? It's the least I can do for being such a klutz."

"That sounds nice, actually. I'm new here and I haven't had a chance to talk to anyone but the family in over a week. My name's Lolly—Lolly Stone," She extended her hand to Landers.

"Hello, Lolly. I'm Mellisa Landers, but my friends all call me Mel. I'm new here, too, and I haven't talked to anyone in more than a week, either. Come on, let's go find a place to sit and chat for a bit."

She was going to miss the shuttle, but it didn't seem important. She could come back again, later in the week—the caverns would still be there, of that she was sure. The opportunity for simple human contact had presented itself, and she was going to take advantage of it.

"So," Lolly Stone said as she buttered the top of her cinnamon roll, "what brings you out here to this place that time and civilization overlooked?"

It didn't take long before the simple human contact she so desperately wanted wandered into uncomfortable territory, and she had to think fast so she could get past it and onto something else without obviously changing the topic. It was a simple and natural question Lolly Stone asked and she should have known it would come up. She decided to be semi-truthful, so her answer wouldn't come out sounding contrived.

"I'm an investigative reporter. A little over a week ago I was talking to an acquaintance from NASA, and he told me I ought to find a hole to hide in. It was a crazy comment, coming from him, but it gave me an idea for a series—a way to get into another area of writing—so I decided to come out here and do a little journalistic piece on the caverns."

"Did you say that a friend from NASA told you to find a hole to hide in?"

"That's right. And he's just an acquaintance, not a friend."

"Friend, acquaintance—doesn't matter. If you wouldn't mind, I'd like you to meet my husband. Want to follow me out to the house?"

"I...don't have a car."

Damn, that was stupid.

"You're a reporter out here to write about the caverns, and you don't have a car?"

"I left mine in Tampa. Thought I'd rent one here," she said. She was sure her discomfort was showing like a sign hanging on her chest. At least she hadn't said anything about coming to Carlsbad on the bus. That would be hard to explain. This way, she thought, Lolly will think I flew out.

Calm down...

"Well, never mind. I can take you out to the house, then I'll run you over to wherever it is you're staying. Does that sound okay?"

"Um, sure, I'd like that." What else could she say? Besides, it would be an opportunity for her to see a little more of the city.

* * *

26 January 2054: 0915 MST

"What do you know about caverns, Scolini?" a voice droned in his earphone. It was one of the operators from Central Dispatch.

Scolini adjusted his earphone and pulled down the boom mic. "What should I know about caverns? I know that they're holes in the ground. That enough?"

"Not quite. Get your ass over to the Director's office—he's got a hot one for you."

"Stone?"

"Nope. Some guy named Klein. Anyway, quick-time it over there. He sounded nervous and you know how he can be when he's nervous."

"Yeah, yeah, yeah...I'm on my way. Don't want the boss man to get a hernia."

* * *

Scolini turned off the main hall and into the office of the Director of Operations. The man seated at the desk, Edwin Holbrook, appeared to Scolini as if he hadn't slept in days. Holbrook didn't look up from the monitor on his desk, just gestured with his hand for Scolini to take a seat and kept on reading for another couple of minutes.

Still concentrating on the monitor, he said, "I have another one for you. This one seems to be important to a lot of people for some reason. Stuff is still coming in on him and his wife, but LA Metro has reason to think that they are headed for the caverns near Carlsbad. I want you to take a few of your people and pour them into park ranger suits. Get them up to the Carlsbad National Park as soon as you can and close down the park, but don't seal it off from the public. If these people intend to use the area near the caverns to hide in, we can use them as a trap. I'll have a cover story to satisfy the people who are working up there, and we'll have them transferred immediately to other parks." Holbrook leaned back in his chair and looked at Scolini with fatigue cluttering his face. "I can't believe how complicated this is getting." He accompanied the comment with an exaggerated sigh.

"Okay. Who is this guy, and what about Stone?"

"Emery Klein is his name. He and his wife are professors and researchers from Cal Western University. His wife bought a book on caverns, an

95

odd thing for an astrophysicist to do, they said, and they failed to show up for some meeting or something. Disappeared from their house a week ago without a word to anyone, and haven't been seen since. The Sector Chief over there is fuming. Oh, and Stone? He's still your baby—and I want him in here soon or you may be out looking for another job along with a few of the rangers."

"I'm working on the Stone thing. Do we have what we need on these Klein people?"

"We have enough. Chips and holos will be in your box when you leave. Got any leads on Stone, yet?"

"No. I was hoping you had something more on him. Something that would give us a direction to look in, at least. You'd think that damned truck—whatever you want to call it—would have been seen somewhere, but we haven't turned up anything on it or his family. And I still think we're being stonewalled by the DoD on this guy. What happened with Worth?"

"Worth?"

"Yeah, Worth, my ex-second."

"Oh, that one. Let's just say that he's no longer with us. Now, get the hell out of my office—and get Stone for me."

* * *

26 January 2054: 1015 MST

Wendell Stone sat quietly, his hands wrapped around a cup of coffee that breathed an aromatic fog into the air, while Mellisa Landers related the conditions that brought her to Carlsbad. From all that he could read in her face, she was not being completely honest, her story was too sketchy and lacked a lot of little details people tend to throw in when they're talking about something they've done.

"Ms. Landers, would you do me a favor and drop your effort to cover up the real reason for you being here? Most of what you've told us is plausible, but it's not the whole thing, and it's not totally straight. I'm sorry about being so blunt, when we've just met, but this is really important, okay?"

Landers moved uncomfortably in her chair. "Well, I...uh, oh, hell.

He...Albert, acted as if he was afraid to be seen in my company, like I was a pariah—that I was somehow going to get him into trouble. Frankly, he scared me to death with his own fear and his comments. I've never known him to act like that."

"What was your story for leaving Tampa?"

"I told Elaine, she's my editor, I had just uncovered new information on the Harrington disappearance—big story of the day, you know— and that I was going under for a while to investigate it. I gave the same story to everyone I know, then got on the bus."

"That's good. It's even believable. Now, let me tell you what this is about."

Wendell Stone spent the next half hour explaining to Landers all that they had uncovered about the coming storm, the Lazarus project and all the details pertaining to it. All the while he kept an eye on her and watched her slowly change from incredulous to shocked, until a certain look of determination grew steadily across her face. From that solid expression, he knew it was time.

"Now, Ms. Landers, what do you think of your Dr. Zweig's behavior."

"Poor...poor Albert. I had no idea. I thought he'd gone off to join the lemmings at the edge of the cliff, but now I see what was gnawing at him, and it's no wonder he was frightened. He was only trying to protect me when he dragged me off to the bar like that."

"There you go, Ms. Landers. No, that's too stiff. May I call you Mellisa?"

"Mel would be better."

"All right, Mel. Dyllan, do you think you can work up a new ID for Mel?"

"Sure. Who would you like to be, Joan of Arc?"

"Definitely not her. I don't like how she ended."

"Now that you're here, and you know all that we do, I think I have a job for you that's tied directly to your background—if you're up for it, that is."

"After what you told me, I'm up for almost anything. What would you like me to do?"

* * *

26 January 2054: 1100 MST

"I'm going to run down to the caverns with

Dan. Anybody want to go with us?" Emery Klein said.

His daughter, Roberta, jumped up from the couch in the living room where she was watching some old cartoon vids with the children and headed for the combination kitchen and dining area of the small house they'd rented under a fictitious name. The house was located in a shallow valley well west of the old city of Carlsbad and was isolated enough that her father thought it would be a safe place for them to stay while they worked out what they would do next.

"You bet," she said. "Anything to get these kids out of this house and out of my hair. They're...driving me crazy and I don't think I can stand another cartoon today—maybe never."

"How about you, Sandy?" he ventured.

"Not today. I want to finish this book first," she said from the recliner in the living room, and gave a lazy wave of her reader. "You don't mind, do you?"

"No, babe. You go ahead and finish your book and we'll bring you back a pocket load of brochure chips to chew on this afternoon," he said. "What are you reading?"

"It's the Spelunker's Guide to Caverns in the Guadalupe Reef Zone.

Very interesting," she replied. "Where did you get that?"

"University Bookstore. Why?"

"Bad choice, Sandy."

"Again...why?"

"Because you may have tipped them off to our whereabouts. Oh well...too late to worry about it.

What about Morgan?"

"No doubt about that. He hates being fenced in—his history, you know. He's out back somewhere, kicking rocks or something. I'll go get him," Roberta Klein said. "Watch the kids for a minute?"

"I'll take that duty," Landers said, and drifted off to the small vid room.

* * *

26 January 2054: 1145 MST

When they got off the elevator, there was hardly anyone in the big room where the snack bar and restrooms were located. Emery counted no more than thirty people, including the group that had come down in the car with them. He felt ill at ease and exposed. He tried to calm himself with the thought that there were only a couple of park rangers and one man working in the snack bar. No need to feel this way, he thought. No goons down here. His daughter and her children disappeared into the restrooms and his brother went with Morgan Hathaway to gawk at the informative animated murals that lined the walls. He went to the snack bar to pick up some goodies for the kids. When he turned to leave the snack bar with two big bags of GummiBats, four large tubs of popcorn jammed in a carry box in one hand and a six pack of sodas in the other, he got no more than three steps back toward the tables. Powerful hands clamped down on both his arms and turned him back toward the elevator.

100

"You will come with us, Professor Klein," the one to his right said in a snarling sort of voice. "Ha! Got us a Camp 32 special, Lou."

"Yeah. How 'bout that, and on our first field assignment. Get a move on, Doc."

Goons dressed up like park rangers. Can't be anything else or they wouldn't have known my name.

Although he was concerned for himself, he was more worried about the others and complied, saying nothing. The elevator door was closing and he could just see his daughter and the kids coming out of the restrooms. He hoped they wouldn't notice him and say or do anything. They didn't. They moved directly to his brother and son-in-law. As the elevator ascended, the man who had not spoken took the things Emery Klein bought at the snack bar and set them on the floor. He was relieved that they didn't bother to count the number of popcorn containers in the box. They pulled his arms in front of him roughly and fixed restraints tightly to his wrists.

"Where is your wife, Professor Klein?"

"My wife is in Mexico. She's doing some research down there. Why?"

"Never mind why. We ask the questions, Doc, and you give us the answers. That's how this works."

"I just told you."

"Wrong. You just lied to us," the snarling one said, and gave him a quick, hard jab to the solar plexus. "Now, where is Mrs. Klein, Professor?"

They exited the elevator at the upper floor and

101

took him to a small room where they tethered him to a pipe. They left him there while they went to bring their car around front. It wasn't easy because the tether was short, but he managed to get one of the sheets off a note pad in his shirt pocket and wrote as fast as he could, then folded it so his monogram showed on both sides—he finished just in time.

* * *

Her father had disappeared and she was running in panic, but not so much that she didn't notice a small scrap of paper on the floor by the door of the lobby. It had her dad's personal monogram on it. She stooped down and picked it up.

"What's that?" Morgan Hathaway asked.

"Note from Dad," she said, unfolding the small piece of paper.

He looked over her shoulder at the writing. "What the hell is that?" he said. "Can you read it?"

"No, but Mom can."

"So can I," Daniel Klein said. "Let me see it."

With trembling hands, she gave the note to her uncle.

He spent a minute reading the note, then said, "Oh, shit. Come on, let's go. We have to move—and move fast."

Chapter 6

Holbrook sat at his desk, staring, unblinking, at the man across from him. He twirled a light pen through his fingers, back and forth in a continuous, monotonous motion. After a couple of minutes of that, he put the pen down and leaned forward.

"I want you to understand, Dr. Klein, that we are at liberty to use whatever means are required to extract the information we want. I believe you have a pretty good idea of what that would mean. I think, if I were you, I would opt for the most painless, non-invasive method. Now, why don't you simply tell me the truth and avoid all the other things that will happen if you don't? You've already had some experience with that from my people, I understand. Where is your wife, your brother, daughter and her husband— and your grandchildren? I promise you that, if you cooperate, they will be treated well."

"Your promise hardly represents any kind of guarantee, does it?"

Klein was the first detainee Holbrook had dealt with and it was proving to be...difficult. He tried to put himself in Klein's shoes and thought about how he would react under similar circumstances. He decided he would probably be frightened for himself and his family. He would probably be reluctant to say anything to jeopardize them and endure as much as he could to keep them free, just as Klein was doing. But Klein, he knew, was aware that there was no way to fight the drugs they would

103

soon use on him if he continued to resist.

"Yes, Dr. Klein, it does. You see, I have what could be called supreme power in my Sector. That means that whatever I say is law here. If I tell my people to eliminate your family when they are found, and they will be, that is exactly what will happen. Now, will you cooperate?"

"What happens if I do?"

"I think you should be inclined to be more concerned about what will happen if you don't."

"I am, believe me, but I still want to have an idea of what I'm being offered here—if you don't mind."

"All right, Dr. Klein. Here is the offer. You cooperate with me and I will guarantee that your family will be treated well and that all of you will be reunited in the same camp. I can't let you go— you, of all people, are in a position to know that."

"Yes, I am, and I do understand what it is you're doing. It's a bag of BS, but I understand what's going on well enough. All right, I'll tell you what I can. Does that sound fair to you?"

"Yes. Go on."

"My wife, Sandy, and I rented a small apartment at the Carlsbad Inn. We were waiting for the kids and my brother to join us there. When I was picked up at the caverns, they hadn't yet shown up. I can't tell you where the others are because I don't know."

"Dr. Klein, you disappeared from your place in LA Metro more than a week ago. You've been in Carlsbad at least a week. The information we have on your daughter and son-in-law is that they also left their residence at about the same time. Right after they received a package from you that was delivered by private courier. Where would they be, if not in Carlsbad?"

"My brother has a restaurant and a couple of houses in Jal, New Mexico. They may still be there."

That was information Holbrook didn't have. Klein's brother represented a segment of society that had rebelled against the Unified System and vanished from the grid three years ago. The antisocial cadre had formed a loosely knit organization, calling itself the Traveler's Society, that was dedicated to keeping each other off the grid and out of sight. They had become...troublesome, and exceptionally efficient. Daniel Klein had not been heard from since. Maybe Emery Klein was telling him the truth.

Maybe.

"Where is this restaurant and what are the addresses of the houses?"

"I've never been out there, so I don't know the addresses, but the name of the restaurant is Tortilla Flats Fiesta. From what Dan told me, Jal is a small town, so he shouldn't be all that hard to find. You know, of course, that he's one of the Travelers and is probably using a different name—and no, I'm afraid I don't know what that is, either."

Well, we're making a little progress here, Holbrook thought.

Everything Klein said was plausible and Holbrook accepted it as containing a seed of truth, for the time being. Klein was scheduled for the next transfer to the special camp at eight-thirty, but he would still be available for further questioning while he was in the building, if needed. Holbrook decided he would live up to his word as much as he could until a hole appeared in Klein's story.

"All right, Dr. Klein. We will be putting you on a bus for the camp in a few minutes, but I must warn you, if anything you've said proves not to be true, you will be questioned by the people at the camp. They are not in a position to offer you anything—only I can do that—and they will use drugs. Once you're in their custody, your fate is out of my hands, which means I can negotiate nothing with you after you leave this facility. Are you absolutely certain there is nothing you would like to add or change?"

* * *

27 January 2054: 0840 MST

"My legs are killing me," Roberta Hathaway said, her voice coarse with the dryness of having slept the night in the tight confines of Daniel Klein's old truck. "I've got to get out of here and stretch the cramps out of them— and breathe some air that hasn't been breathed by somebody else first. No offense, Dan, but the air purifier and humidifier in your truck aren't working."

Morgan Hathaway opened the door and climbed out into a cheek reddening wind. He did a couple of deep knee bends, then helped his wife extract her stiff body from the cab.

"Not too surprising when you think about how old it is—that thing's almost fifty. Hell, I'm surprised it still runs," her husband said.

"I guess. Good grief, is it colder today, or is it my imagination?" She reached over and closed the door as quietly as possible so she wouldn't awaken the children who were sleeping comfortably in the back seat, buried in a mountain of snuggle-warm quilt.

"It's colder, Bobby," her uncle said, coming around to join them, his words being blown away in little gray puffs on the wind. "What we need to do now is find another place to stay, a place where we won't be noticed. Then I'll start thinking on what we can do about Em."

"I don't know that there's anything we can do," Sandra Klein said, as she joined the group. Her voice was stern, curt, and filled with depression. She had cried herself through the night, and she knew the results could be seen by everyone, but she didn't care. They had taken her Em, and she was both angered and overloaded with sadness by what had become a bad dream awake.

"We...we don't know what they'll do or where they intend to take him. I wish I'd gone into mechanical engineering like I'd planned, instead of letting him talk me into astrophysics so we'd share a lot of the same classes. No, that's not true. I wouldn't change anything, except what's happening now. Where do you suggest we start looking for a place to stay?"

"While we were driving out here, I noticed that a bunch of these places are vacant—more than

107

not—and have been for a long time. I think we could get away with claiming squatter's rights almost anywhere. Any one of these little valleys would be fine as long as it's out of town—what town there is— and away from other people," Daniel Klein said. "From what I've seen, there aren't any people out here to be away from. What about heat and light?"

"You leave that to your old uncle Dan, sweetheart. I know how to take care of those things."

All of them came to the same conclusion at about the same time. It was better being warm, cramped, and breathing each other's air than it was to be freezing. As they were climbing back into the truck, Sandra Klein took hold of her brother-in-law's arm and turned him away from the door.

"Do you believe there's anything we can do for Em?"

"To tell you the truth, sis, I don't know. Later, after we're in some place and it's working, I'll take a run down to the caverns—alone—to see if I can find out anything."

"Why alone? Why can't I go with you?" She wanted to feel like she was taking an active part in getting her husband back and she wanted go with him. Doing anything would be better than just waiting to know the worst.

"Because I dropped off their radar a while back. I'm a nonperson, remember? No pictures, no prints of any kind—I don't exist. Em may have to give them some info, but he doesn't know what identity I'm using, so they won't be able to get that out of him. He'll probably have to tell them where I am—well, was—but they won't be able to find out anything beyond that, and nobody in Jal knows anything more than what I told them, and that was a lot of BS that will only confuse them more. The rest of you are in their current files."

* * *

"Uh-oh. We have company."

"ISA?"

"Not unless they've taken to requisitioning their vehicles from the Smithsonian. Anyway, we're safe in here and Carolyn knows what to do. Want to take a look?" Wendell put down the seismic sensor they were working on and walked over to Drake's security monitor. On the screen was an old, beat up pickup truck full of people. It was hard to see any detail through the mud and ice covered windows, but there appeared to be four adults and two small children inside. The door on the driver's side opened and a big man stepped down. Through the open door Wendell could see the people in the cab clearly.

"I recognize that woman, Dyllan. This may be a weird and...maybe...lucky break for us."

"Oh, yeah? Who is she?"

"One of the people I told you about from Cal Western University. She's an astrophysicist. I don't see her husband in there, but he's a meteoriticist and both of them know about the Lazarus program."

"Maybe it would be wise not to show your face. Just in case, you know."

109

"Doesn't matter if I show my face or not. Lolly's in the house with Carolyn and the Klein woman is bound to recognize her. Come on, let's get over there and see why someone who makes more than two grand a week is riding around in that remnant tank of days gone by in a broad valley of ghosts."

* * *

All of the adults were gathered around the dining room table and the two children were engrossed in old recorded cartoons on the vid in the living room. Stone and Drake listened while Sandra Klein explained what had happened at the caverns and how her daughter had found the note by the entry to the upper level lobby.

"May I see the note?"

"Sure, but it's in Hebrew," she said, and retrieved it from her bag. Stone smiled and took the note from her. He read it through carefully, then turned his attention to Drake, who was sitting in the corner, tinkering with a new holopad.

"Dyllan, we need to get back in—now."

"Too soon," he said without looking up. "They'll detect the intrusion and shut down my pathway. Then, they'll change their damned encryptions. It'll take a week of work to get back in."

"You told me you were going to wait a week to go back in, anyway. What's the big deal?"

"The work, man. Okay, okay, we pay them a visit now. What are we looking for?"

"Camp numbers and locations in whatever they're calling this sector. Anything to do with population type. They'll probably segregate them for control purposes. Government thinking. I want layouts, if possible, and, if you have time, download anything else you can get your hands on about this sector before they shut you out. Particularly Special Camp 32. You're the King of Hackerdom, remember?"

Drake looked up from his little project and frowned. "You're not thinking about trying to get him out, are you?"

"I don't know. Not yet, anyway."

"You are. Yes...you are. I can see it running around in your empty skull. You're nuts, you know that, Wendell? What the hell do you think we can do? Look around you. Do we look like an experienced strike team?

Only two of us have the knowhow to pull that kind of stunt, and I'm not interested."

"Sometimes it's best to go in with minimum numbers."

"One?"

"Damn it," Daniel Klein remarked, "I should have known that wasn't a word in his note. I forgot about the old numbering system."

"So did I," Sandra Klein said.

Stone turned back to the group at the table and fixed his gaze on Mrs. Klein. "We're all on the same sinking ship here, so is it all right with you if I call you Sandy?"

"Of course."

"All right, Sandy, tell me all you can about

111

what you've deduced from the figures you have on this cometary flux and any damage estimates you may have made."

"Em did most of that. We talked about it a lot, though, so I'll tell you whatever I can remember. Mars and the moon will do better, barring a direct strike. Very little atmosphere on Mars to retain the ejecta in—fallout should be rather fast there—and no atmosphere on the moon. I can tell you right away that it doesn't look good for anyone anywhere on this planet, though. "

"What does, these days?"

* * *

27 January 2054: 1140

An old man pushed hard against the door to the lobby until it opened just enough for him to squeeze through. He was dressed in a ragged camouflage shirt, khaki pants, dull combat boots, and a wool, navy blue watch cap pulled down over his ears, his long white hair spewing from beneath it in all directions the way snow does in a whirlwind. His full, white beard did the same. He hobbled toward the park ranger standing near the upper level restrooms, his thick, black cane tapping hard against the floor as he shuffled with what appeared to be great effort toward the men's room.

He stopped in front of the ranger.

"How far down to the bottom of the elevator, sonny?" he asked. The old man watched as the ranger's gaze wandered quickly to the wall where

112

some of the cavern's stats were displayed.

"Um, 230 meters, sir."

"Uh-huh," the aged man responded. He raised his cane and pointed it at the agent's chest. "Rough night, bad morning, or a little bit of both?"

"What do you mean?"

"Forgot to put on your name tag, sonny."

"Oh, yeah, that. Well—"

"This here cane's a 16 gauge, loaded with double-aught, and it's primed and ready to spray your innards all over the wall behind you."

"What the hell is this—?"

"Just shut up and walk this old timer out to his car like a good boy. Can't have old folks like me walking around in a dangerous place like this alone, can we? Never know what I might run into, huh?"

When they reached the ancient pickup truck, the old man jammed the cane against the base of the ranger's skull.

"Now, be a good fella and put your hands behind your back. We're gonna fit you with some nice, new bracelets—don't so much as twitch or your head is hamburger."

Once the restraints were in place, the old man drew a sack down over the ranger's head and pulled the drawstring in around his throat. Then he opened the rear door of the truck's cab.

"There, that's better, sonny. Can't have you seeing where you're going, can we? Now climb on up in the back seat here and lie down on the floor. You and I are going for a little ride."

The truck turned left onto the old, pockmarked, broken highway and headed off toward Carlsbad.

113

The elderly man had not said a word since leaving the parking lot. About three kilometers north of the White's City cutoff, he looked down at the ranger for the first time.

"How does it feel?"

"What? What are you talking about?"

"How does it feel to be one of the first POWs in this war? Can't say you're the first, because I don't know what's happening in other places, but you're definitely one of the early ones."

"What war?"

"The us against them war, that's what war. The ISA and whatever other governmental organizations there are around the world working against the people who live on this planet. That war. Now do you know what I mean?"

"No, and what's this ISA thing? I don't know anything about any ISA."

"Sure you do, sonny. Sure you do."

"No, I swear. I work for the National Park Service and...and I was just assigned to the Caverns last week."

"You were sent here no earlier than yesterday, sonny, and you don't work for the National Park Service any more than I do."

* * *

27 January 2054: 1150 MST

"Scolini, I just got word that one of your men disappeared from the Caverns. Is he a good one, or is he like Worth?"

114

"Yeah, I just heard about that, and he's a good one."

"Well, what happened to him?"

"I don't know, yet. Maybe a hot date with one of the rangerettes? I just sent a team up there and I'll be going up in about an hour."

"Good. Find him and get it figured out. And where the hell is Stone?"

"Don't know yet, sir, but I'm working on it."

"Well, stop working on it and start getting him. That man I want in a cell or a bag...and the sooner, the better."

Scolini flipped up his mic, looked across the desk at his new second officer and frowned. What the hell does Holbrook think I am, a magician? he thought.

"Do we have anything new on Stone?"

"No, and every time I start asking about him I run into a brick wall.

What's with this guy that they want to protect him so much?"

"I don't know and I've given up caring. The boss man's about to go into orbit and that means my job is getting closer to the edge of the cliff every minute that we don't have Stone, but I have an idea that might help. It's still cold up there where his house is, but there's been plenty of sun the last couple of days. The snow's starting to melt off, so there's bound to be some track where the stuff got packed down under that monster he was driving that the radar should pick up as a density differential. If we can find the direction he went we can at least get a handle on where he might have gone. We know he wasn't on the highway, so we check the ground around the area. Get on it and I'll go over to get a flyer readied for us. We have to run up to the Caverns and check on our missing man."

Chapter 7

"Look, General Stoker, it's a simple matter of calling off your hounds in the El Paso office. This man, you have him in your records as Wendell Stone, has sensitive information that we can't afford to have leaked to anyone. He apparently knows your people are after him and, as a result, he's effectively vanished. He knows how to work silent and underground better than any man alive and that means there's no way anyone, not even our best, will find him."

Stoker fiddled nervously with some things on his desk. Project Lazarus was his baby, that was true on the surface, but not in reality, and he had little direct control over what the field offices were doing. They would follow his specific orders, of course, but no information from the field offices was fed to the home office in the Pentagon unless there was an overwhelming reason. It was obvious the people in El Paso didn't feel that what they were doing with the Stone case was of any interest to him—or his staff. And what was this sensitive information Stone was toting?

"Sounds to me like you have this man on a string. Why don't you reel him in?"

"We had him on a string...and I wish it were that simple, but, unfortunately, it was a loose string, and now it's broken. Technically, he still works for us, even though he's been allowed to leave the service. We've been keeping a casual watch on him

117

for a few years, but now he's nowhere in sight. For us, that's a dangerous turn of events and we want him to come back in. He won't do that as long as he feels he's at risk from your Lazarus thugs."

"Thugs?"

"All right, agents, if you prefer. Whatever you want to call them, they're free to do as they damn well please—and you know what that can lead to. I suggest that you come up with something that will enable you to maintain tighter control over those people in the field and I—we—want you to back off of Stone."

"All right. I will do what I can. Is that all?"

"No. For your information, Stone probably knows everything there is to know about Lazarus by now, and he has a sad penchant toward social responsibility and idealism. He's what they used to call a patriot. If he gets it in his mind that this murky little program of yours is not beneficial to society, and we both know it's not, he'll do anything he can to bring it down and expose all the participants, including the president. After that, we have anarchy and panic in the streets. It could even lead to the end of Operation Rebirth."

"But...that's impossible."

"Is it, now?"

"You make him sound like some kind of superhuman."

"Let's put it this way, he wasn't chosen because he was slow and witless, and he wasn't kept on our list of operatives because we like him. He's not superhuman, but if anyone ever came close to qualifying for that sort of recognition, he's the

118

one. You just call off the dogs and we'll do what we can to bring him in, once he's satisfied that the heat's off. For all anyone knows, it may already be too late."

"All this over one man sounds a little ridiculous, to me."

"He's not one man. He's an entire division rolled into one. You know, there were some films made a long time ago about an ex-Green Beret. What the hell was his name? Um—"

"Rambo?" Stoker offered. He remembered the character well—one of his childhood heroes.

"Rambo, that's the one. Stone makes Rambo look like a thumb- sucking, kindergarten dropout with an IQ of one. Back off—and do it now."

"All right, but there is nothing I can do about the ISA and they've taken a keen interest in him, too. You'll have to talk directly to the Geek Brigade to get them to back down."

* * *

29 January 2054: 0745 MST

Scolini rubbed the sleep from his eyes as he stumbled down the hall to the dining area of the apartment they had taken to serve as an on-site operations office at the west end of White's City. On the table in the kitchenette there were several monitors and keypads. One of the operators looked up from his monitor as Scolini entered.

"We have established a tentative track for that Stone vehicle," he said. "It's patchy, at best, and disappears completely about fifty klicks east of a little place called Engle. He appears to have been heading for White Sands."

"Punch up the map and let's have a look," Scolini said as he poured out a cup of coffee from the brewer on the kitchen counter and grabbed a couple of doughnuts out of a box next to the machine. "It doesn't figure that he'd go into a military reservation that is crawling with government personnel. Superimpose the projected track on the map."

The operator laid the radar projection on the map and extended the line in a different color from the point where the tracks were lost. It went straight through White Sands. Scolini stood, looking at the monitor, and shaking his head slowly.

"No," Scolini said. "He wouldn't have done that, and I doubt he'd want to backtrack too much, either. No. He has to have turned east, somewhere along that line. We know he wouldn't have taken any of the automateds because we'd know where he went. Delete all the highways that are currently on the grid and let's see what we have left."

The operator tapped a few keys and all the controlled highways faded to light gray traces. "Okay," Scolini said, his mouth full of glazed doughnut. "See that? Only highways 54, 70, 82, 180, 285, and 380 aren't tied to the system in the area where his tracks were lost. His possible destinations of any size at all, without having to get on the grid, are Tularosa, Alamogordo, Artesia, Las Cruces, El Paso, Hobbs, and—well, I'll be damned—Carlsbad! Could it be that Stone came here? Right here under our noses? What are the odds against that?"

29 January 2054: 0800 MST

"Mommy, Jason won't stop kicking me under the covers," Lisa, the seven year-old, said from the living room.

Roberta excused herself from the table where a fine breakfast spread had been laid out by Carolyn and Lolly, and headed for the scene of battle. "You'd better have stopped that by the time I get in there, young man, or I'm going to paddle your behind," she said.

"As I see it," Wendell said, smiling at Roberta's retreating figure, "we're going to need all the help we can get, and we're going to have to find some TS people who are willing to lend a hand."

"TS people? What are TS people?" Sandra said.

"He's talking about the Travelers Society," Dan told her. "Like me."

"You're a Traveler?" Wendell said, looking up from his plate of chopped bacon and scrambled eggs.

"Yep. I'm surprised you hadn't figured that out already."

"Do you know any others around here?"

"No, not here, but I'm sure there must be some. I know a couple up in Artesia, and they probably know a few folks down here we can contact."

"Good. How about running up there to find out

121

what they know?"

"As good as done. Um, what do you need with Travelers?"

"You people can move around without ringing any bells. We need local eyes and ears, and we're going to need as much help as we can find to do what we have to do to gain access to those caverns and do all the construction it'll take to make them as safe as we can. It's not going to be easy with them watching. I know it was unintentional, but we've broadcast a possible intention to use the Caverns and we know they're sitting on them now. Dyllan can fix us up with communications no one can tap into."

"I can?"

"Yes, you can—and I think the sooner you get to work on that, the better."

"Wait a minute," Sandra said. "I'm lost here. Dan, what is this Travelers Society?"

"I don't have enough time to explain it all, Sis, but we don't exist. Not officially, anyway. We all jump off the grid and our records get erased and replaced. A lot of us have several different identities in the system that we can use to get us through control sites. I'll tell you about it when I get back. All right if I take Jerry along?"

"No, not yet."

"Aw, Dad. I've been here forever with nothing to do but watch those dumb old cartoons."

"No, Jerry, and that's that. I have my reasons. If you want something to do, I have a job I've been thinking about for a few days that's right up your alley, kiddo. Come on out to the barn and I'll show

122

you what I want. We can feed our ranger while we're at it. Still have that blank, Dyllan?"

"Yeah. If I remember correctly, the whole damned kit's out there in my pile of things-I'm-going-to-do-someday, when-I-get-around-to-it. I managed to get the machine and the yoke together, though, so those parts are set to go. All the concrete and steel work is completed for the yoke's base structure, too. That's what's in the shed on the hill. Nobody would ever know it's an observatory. I guess that's important now, isn't it?"

"Yeah, it is. I remember when you bought it. About four years ago, wasn't it?"

"Has it been that long?"

"What...what about Em?" Sandra said.

"Please, Sandy, I haven't forgotten about Emery and, believe me, we will do whatever we can to get him back for you. We, as a group, need him here, but we just can't go around indiscriminately rattling chains, yet. We're working up a plan. Trust me, okay?"

"All right, Wendell. You seem to know what you're doing, so I'll give you the benefit of the doubt...but I want...him back." Tears were beginning to work their way into her eyes again and she turned away.

* * *

29 January 2054: 0840 MST

Emery drew the light wool ascot he was wearing up over his nose to keep the wind from driving needles into his nasal passages that mercilessly pounded his sinuses with a sharp pain. He joined the other six passengers, two older men and four women, where they stood in a small group in the sally port, stamping their feet in an effort to stay warm. He thought he recognized one of the women as Gerta Windaus, a world renown comet hunter from McDonald Observatory in Texas. Above them and to their left stood a tall tower. Inside the glass cage at the top of the tower a couple of uniformed men watched them, and the concrete ring at the base of their enclosure bristled with the barrels of auto-controlled lasers, all trained on their little group. He pushed his hands farther down into his pockets.

Inside the inner fence line he could see no one. Were they the first to have been brought to this place in the middle of what appeared to be endless flat sand until it collided with low mountains on all sides? Some small structures pierced the horizon line to the south and east, but, as far as he could tell, there was nothing else around. The sign over the gate said simply:

"WELCOME TO SPECIAL CAMP 32"

Yeah, right. Welcome. The only thing missing is, 'Arbeit Macht Frei,' and what the hell is the meaning of "Special"?

"Excuse me," he said as he approached the woman he thought he recognized. "Are you Dr. Windaus?"

"Yes...and you are?"

"Emery Klein from Western U."

"It appears," she began, "that we will all be meeting colleagues, known and unknown, soon, Dr.

124

Klein. Odd that a travesty of justice like this could have produced such a profoundly positive side effect, is it not? I read your book on impact mechanics and its associated effects on geomorphology—it was an excellent work."

"Thank you. Does anyone have any idea where we are?"

"Yes," one of the elderly men responded. "I had the pleasure of working out here for several years. We're in the White Sands Missile Range, not too far from a region where the first fission weapon was tested. They call the place the 'Trinity Site'. Ha! They sought to keep us from knowing where we were, then brought me to the very place I worked for thirty years. So much for the blacked out windows in the bus, eh?" He laughed, again, and it came out as a short, hollow, and nervous chuckle, such as a man might do on the way to his execution.

"Yeah. How far is it to the nearest highway?"

"Hard to say. We're anywhere from 40 to 50 kilometers west of Alamogordo...I'd guess. It could be a little farther. I Never paid much attention to distances out here—I never paid much attention to anything out here, to tell you the truth, but the basic terrain is burned into my memory. I hated this place. Now, here I am...again, eh?" He waved an arm at the surrounding desert and frowned.

"Whatever this place is," Windaus began," we are going to have to make the best of it, aren't we?" she said, nodding toward the menacing tower. She looked off to her right, into the huge compound, and shrugged. "Well, at least we are not completely alone, here comes the welcoming committee, my

125

friends."

A small bus pulled up to the inner gate and three men emerged. Two of them were carrying weapons and dressed in dark gray uniforms. The third, a gangly, awkward-looking man in a long, beige overcoat, its collar flipped up to protect his neck from the cold wind, stepped down from the bus and motioned to the guards in the tower. The inner sally port gate opened and he approached the knot of people huddled together in the lee of the larger bus that had brought them to this place. Emery thought he should know the man, but couldn't place him.

"Good morning, my friends," he said as he came closer. The sound of his voice was familiar, too, and Emery felt that, perhaps, things were not going to be as bad as he had thought, though he still couldn't attach an identity to the approaching figure.

"I have been appointed Director of Special Camp 32," he said in an amiable tone. "My name is Fred Lathrop, and it is my job to make sure your stay here is as pleasant as it can be. That is, under the circumstances.

Please, let's get out of this refrigerator and I will explain what will be happening here on our way to the cafeteria. The crew there has, I'm told, prepared a wonderful breakfast for us."

Fred Lathrop, of course, Emery thought. Lathrop had the look of a man in his early fifties, in spite of being in his mid-seventies now. He had been the man in charge of the first colony program back in the mid-thirties, a time when the United

126

States was scrambling to regain some respect in the world after the Japanese successfully landed their people at Pavonis and set up the first viable colony on Mars. The Russians and Chinese followed suit only weeks behind the Japanese, and the Indian ship made orbit about a year and a half later. During that time, the United States was still trying to get off the pad after several setbacks and a couple of disastrous failures.

What a time that was. It had been Lathrop's youthful energy and diplomatic guile that made it possible, a bit over two years later, for the US to set up their own base at Olympus Mons and not have everyone at each other's throats. At the outset, everyone out there was intent on establishing sovereignty over the whole planet and Lathrop became a hero in the space business by, almost singlehandedly, hammering the Martian Cooperative Alliance into place. What, Emery wondered, had brought him to this?

* * *

29 January 2054: 0900

"All right, people, here's what we have. We know there was a connection made between Stone and Klein just days after Lazarus went up. Klein was picked up right over there in that big hole in the ground. What look like Stone's tracks were headed this way, right? So, we're going to look at every shed, shanty, barn, house, hotel, motel and under every rock between here and the far north end of

Old Carlsbad." Scolini began pacing nervously. "We're going to need more people up here or it'll take us forever to do that. Wilkins, get us fifty more trained people up here in a hurry. I want this to be organized and methodical. No mistakes and nothing overlooked."

"Are you sure he's up here?" his second said.

"No, I'm not sure—but it's a damn sight better possibility than anything else we've been able to come up with. Oh, and make sure everyone is armed and has a current holo of Stone and company. If you have to, shoot him, and that goes for his son and his bitch of a wife, too. That order comes straight from the boss man's mouth."

Although he didn't say it, Scolini was certain he'd find the whole bunch of them together— probably all hiding under the same rock. A twisted smile traveled across his face and disappeared as quickly as it had appeared.

"We can't afford to spend a lot of time doing this, people, so don't bother with opening doors. IR scans will be good enough, and if you find so much as warm water in a drain, I want to know about it. A lot of the stuff we're going to be looking at will be off the road, so take the needed vehicles from the park's motor pool. And be careful, this Stone guy is supposed to be as dangerous as they come and, they tell me, slippery. If you find anything, don't approach unless you know you've got the advantage. Just call it in and sit on it until you have some backup. Now, go assemble your teams and check back here to get your search areas and orders before you leave. I don't want a lot of unnecessary

128

radio in the field, so we're going offline as of right now."

"So, how do we call in if we're offline?" one of the men said. "There will be flyers up for laser-com relays. Again—no radio."

* * *

29 January 2054: 1030 MST

"Listen to me, Holbrook...we want you to stand down from this Stone thing, and that's all there is to it."

"But, Colonel, I don't..."

"No excuses. You get off Stone's butt, and you get off it now."

The image on the screen, Colonel Lionel Packwood, Chief of Operations for Lazarus Sector, was glowering at Holbrook now. What could he say? Did he dare tell Packwood that Scolini and his team had taken themselves offline to keep their activities undetected? It appeared to Holbrook that he had no choice.

"Colonel, the team in Carlsbad is...offline. We are aware of Stone's fabled abilities and, in view of that, the agent in charge opted to go silent. We can't talk to them at this time."

"Then send up a flunky to talk to him directly. Go up there yourself— even if you have to walk. We, and that means all of us, want Stone left alone for the time being. This is a high priority matter. Do I make myself clear?"

"Quite clear, Colonel. I'll have a courier up

129

there in an hour. I have to advise you, however, that I don't know what their plans are and it may take a while to make contact."

"We both know better than that, Holbrook. If they've gone silent, then they're light talking and that means they have a couple of relay units hovering in the area. You send a flyer up there with sensors and you find them. You have two and a half hours to do it and report back to me. Two and a half hours, Holbrook, and I want to be listening to good news or you'll be joining our guests in one of the camps."

Was the son-of-a-bitch smiling at him—or sneering? Holbrook couldn't decide which. The screen went blank without so much as a "Good-bye" and Holbrook was on the line to dispatch without a second's hesitation. What is it this guy Stone has going for him?

* * *

29 January 2054: 1142 MST

Scolini chewed viciously at his cigar while he listened to the secured incoming message from the El Paso office. Stone had become a fixation for him and he wasn't going to give up so easily. That much he knew. He would find a way to continue the search for Stone in another way. When the message from El Paso concluded, he had his answer ready. He reached down and switched on the radio to speak directly to the pilot of the flyer from El Paso. That, he thought, should convince them that I'm cooperating.

"Acknowledged. We are to stand down on Stone. Relay to Director Holbrook that I understand and will comply, but that we will remain in the area for the time being. We have reason to believe that Sandra Klein and the rest of the family are still here and we will begin our sweep for them in the morning. We should have them in custody in about two weeks—or less, if we're lucky. Scolini, out."

That should do it—and he would still be able to hunt for Stone without Holbrook's knowledge. Now, the priorities were shifted a little. He would have to dispose of Stone and his people without reporting that it had been done. He would pick a select group of agents to do the hunting and keep them separated from the rest, give them a "shoot to kill" order, then wait for the results. It was a big area and it was going to take longer than he liked—but he would find them and erase them from his database.

After all, who's going to know? I knock off Stone and family, dump their carcasses in one of these ravines out here and eliminate any agents involved in that part of it. Then I write the agents off as resulting from field actions with the Stones. They were hostile and resisted. Yeah. All neat and clean. I get rid of the Klein clan the same way so there won't be any contradictions in the reports. Yeah, I like that. Now, all I have to do is find them—and it doesn't matter to me in what order. Hell, I might even get promoted for the Klein thing because they're supposed to be a hot item, too.

Chapter 8

Dan Klein's ancient truck skidded off the gravel road, roared up the long drive, and ground to a shuddering stop in front of the house. He jumped down from the cab and ran to the front door where Lolly and Jeremy Stone greeted him.

"Why the big rush?" Lolly said. "Where's Wendell?"

"Out in the barn with Dyllan and Sandy. Why? What's happened?"

"A lot has happened—and is happening. Call them down here—we need to talk."

* * *

After Roberta managed to get the children peacefully occupied in a game on the internal system, a major feat of diplomacy and outright bribery, they all gathered at the dining room table. Carolyn brought coffee and hot biscuits with chipped beef gravy to the table and took a seat.

"All right, Dan, what's up?" Wendell said.

"Good news, and bad. To the good, seven Traveler families live in this area and the people in Artesia have contacted them through their secured local net. They should be arriving here sometime this afternoon. Now, the bad news. They didn't have a name to hang on those creeps until we talked, but they know that the ISA has moved all the park personnel out and that they're closing the

132

caverns..."

"Bad news? I'd say that's a move in the right direction," Wendell said. "What? How's that possible? If they close the park, we can't use the caverns."

"Wrong, Dan. If they close the park, we can use them. The rangers are familiar with everything there is to know about the caverns and they're dedicated to protecting and preserving the environment, but the ISA isn't— and they have no interest in learning anything about them, either. That means they won't be down there nosing around or trying to preserve anything. They'll probably just lock the doors up top and close off the road to the caverns. Then, they'll vacate the immediate area because they'll think there's no reason to stay up there. We can start our walling off projects years ahead of what we had thought. Pure advantage—all the way around."

"If you say so."

"What about Em?" Sandra asked.

"After we've had a chance to discuss the situation with Dan's friends, we'll know a lot more about that, I hope."

"You hope? You hope? I want Em back. Hope is nice—but it doesn't cut it."

"Don't worry. We've been working up a plan, like I told you before, but we need people we can trust who can move around without drawing attention to themselves to pull it off. Just a few more days, all right?"

"What is a few more days?"

"I can't put a number on it, but it will be soon."

"It had better be."

133

"What if the ISA decides to turn the park back over to the rangers?" Dan said.

"I'm guessing they won't do that. They know we have an interest in the caverns and they're not stupid—no matter what you might think of them—so they'll assume others will come to the same conclusion we did. No, they'll close off access to the caves and set up a loose cordon around the area to prevent anyone else from getting in. After a month or so, they'll get cocky and sloppy about the perimeter. They'll pull in what troops they have out there to use for other things and concentrate the remainder on the main access route down near White's City; pretty standard stuff for the 'Let's-keep-it-efficient,' government mentality."

Stone turned his attention to Mel.

"We have some detail to put on that job I told you we had for you. We're working on a way to hijack the broadcast satellites, but Dyllan says we won't be able to keep the connection longer than five minutes. Sandy's been putting together an animation that shows what's going to happen and I'd like you to work with her on a three to five minute spot to warn people about what they're going to be looking at in a few years—and give them some basic information on how to get themselves ready. But don't forget, the most time we'll have available to us is five minutes—if you can do it in less time, that'll be even better, and it has to be as convincing as you can make it without being so frightening that it causes people to panic. You know what I mean, right? Play up the time they have available to prepare and play down the gory

134

details as much as you can without watering down the importance of the situation too much, but make it obvious that they need to begin soon. Think you can handle that?"

"It's what I do. Sure, I can handle it. Want anything in there about how the government's giving them the royal shaft?"

"Not this time, Mel. The broadcast will probably put that thought in their heads, anyway, if it's not already there."

"All right. How many people do you think we'll reach?"

"We can't say for sure. According to Dyllan, maybe a billion—possibly more. He's rigging it so there will be an automatic download to the whole grid and he's going to code it to take advantage of the satellites' onboard translators to handle the language problem."

"A mere billion is a far cry from the entire population."

"It's enough. Word of mouth will take care of the rest of it. Hell, it's the best shot we have, and we don't think we'll be able to do any more."

"Okay. I guess I'd better get my hair done."

"No need to do that. This will be voice and animation only—digitized voice so it'll work better in the translators—and you won't be seen. Sorry about that, but there's no sense putting you in a worse position than you're already in. It's still a possibility that they're not looking for you, so no bylines, either."

* * *

Standing room only. The house was overflowing with people, most of them just curious about what was happening and anxious for any news of these things coming at them from space. Stone was occupied with an elderly gentlemen, Xavier Martin, who seemed to know everything there was to know about southwestern New Mexico. Another fellow, Robin Stahl, who had been called down from his home north of Roswell was with them. He was ex-military, Army Ranger, and fit in with what Stone needed to do.

Dyllan and Emery's brother, Dan, were there, too.

"Mr. Martin, do they have a medevac unit here in Carlsbad?" Stone asked.

"Yes, they do. The hospital here was moved over to the new city center about eight years ago, but it is accessible. Why?"

"I need a helicopter and someone who can fly it—willing or not."

"Hey, we can do a lot better than a little medevac chopper," Stahl injected.

"Oh?"

"Yeah. What would you say to a Firefly H-29-T, fully armed and stealth equipped? We can take out the towers with it and go straight into the yard to pick up your people. The thing was designed to carry fifteen armed and outfitted troops, so it can handle twenty, maybe a couple more, civilians. No need for ground ops."

"Where the hell would you get that?"

"The Guard armory outside Roswell. They

136

have three of them. You fly?"

"Not helos. Fixed wing, yeah, but I don't trust anything that has to beat the air into submission to get off the ground."

"Weird. A guy with your background has probably spent more time in choppers than most anybody else."

"Yeah, well, spending time in them doesn't mean I enjoyed a minute of it. Um...Roswell's a little far from here."

"That's not a problem. I can get it for you and load it up with a few drums of JP-8 that we'll need for the run we're going to have to make."

"How long before it would be noticed?" Stone didn't miss the idea that Stahl had included himself in the mission. Good, he'll come in handy—and he can fly the damned thing, he thought.

"Minimum of a month and a half. Their air wing is still playing in that fracas over in Turkey. It may never be noticed if you can get this situation to come unglued."

"And you're sure you can fly it?"

"Oh, yeah. With my eyes closed."

"Great. You get the helo as soon as you can, and I can continue with what needs to be done here. When can you get it?"

"Tonight. Better at night. Do you have a place to put it? Can't pick it up on radar but a sensitive IR will see it until it cools down—sort of."

"Yeah—in the barn at the rear."

"Um...excuse me."

"What is it, Dyllan?"

"If I remember correctly, the Firefly is

137

equipped with a pretty fair cloaking system, but it doesn't work up top, so in flight you'll be a nice, visible target. You're going to have to time this so no S-SATs will be over you...or your ass is grass, man."

"Forgot about that. So, get the orbits on the S-SATs for this week and we'll make it work. Oh, and Dyllan, do what you can to get the latest on the number of people they have in that camp and what their schedules are, okay?"

* * *

30 January 2054: 1345 MST

Fred Lathrop pushed his chair back a little and laid his heels comfortably on the desktop. He peered over the top of his narrow reading glasses at Emery Klein.

"I want you to understand, Dr. Klein, that I had to talk myself blue— lay it on a bit heavy in some spots—to get assigned to this camp. I am under no illusion about what it is they intend to do and, frankly, I disagree with them, their methods, and their whole damned plan. It's full of places where things can go wrong...fast—and the bloody thing is as unethical and immoral as you can get."

"Why are you telling me this?"

"Hold on—we'll get to that as soon as I take care of some other business on the agenda today. Now, I received an order from El Paso this morning to run you through an interrogation to determine if you have been truthful in your statements. Would you care for a cup of coffee?"

"Um...yeah...I guess."

"Smoke?"

"Sure. They took mine in El Paso and, as much as I hate to admit it, I really am an addict."

Lathrop stood and began pacing behind his desk.

"Good. Feel free to help yourself to what I have in the box on my desk, and I'll see to it that you have some to take back to your quarters." Lathrop tapped in intercom. "Alba...would you please bring in a couple of cups of your special brew?"

"What...what is this leading up to, Mr. Lathrop."

"Your interrogation, of course. They expect me to ply the truth out of you with drugs—so we're taking care of that part of it now. There's nothing like a little caffeine and nicotine to loosen the lips of the most difficult cases, wouldn't you agree?"

"Ah. I...I think I understand. Why are you doing this?"

"Because, like you, I truly do not agree with their plans, and this is the most...shall we say...effective and convenient way for an old fart like me to fight back. I don't have enough years left to me nor piss and vinegar in my system to jump in their faces like I used to. Now, shall we get down to the interrogation?"

* * *

30 January 2054: 1515 MST

139

"We've just been swept with low level radar from up top," Dyllan said. "Damn. Nothing ever goes the way you want it to. Any ideas?"

"No. Except maybe blow them out of the sky?"

"Wouldn't solve anything. They've already reported us, no doubt."

"Good thing everybody else has gone."

"Yeah...and that gives me an idea."

"Well, let's hear it, Mr. Genius that you are."

"We know they didn't pick up anything from the barn. The only vehicle out there is Dan's truck and it should be cold by now. They probably picked up on the heat from the house and that means they'll send a team over here to check out the house, right?"

"Yeah. So?"

"Is there any way to get everyone except Mel out of there and up here to the barn without being seen?"

"No. Even if they're not seen, the goons will read the residual heat from their trail, but there's a small cellar that was used by the original owner for storage. We've never used it for anything and the door is under the couch in the living room. If we get everyone down there and Mel turns up the heat, they won't register on the portables those creeps probably have. What do you think?"

"I think it's the only chance we have to get out of this without a fight and letting all of them know where we are."

* * *

The knock on the door was politely soft, but firm. Mel opened it and found herself staring into the faces of three stern-looking men dressed in the black uniforms she remembered from the depot in El Paso, including the weapons.

"Yes?"

"Excuse us, ma'am. We're from the New Mexico State Public Safety Agency and we've received a report of a dangerous felon on the loose in the area. Have you seen anything or anyone suspicious out here?"

"No. No, not really—but then I've been busy writing and I probably wouldn't have noticed, anyway."

"You're a writer?"

"Yeah. Well, I like to think of myself as one, anyway."

"Awfully warm in here, isn't it?"

"Not for me. I came up here from Tampa not too long ago and I don't handle the cold all that well yet. For me, this is comfortable. You guys care for some coffee before you go back out into the cold?"

"Uh...no ma'am. What is it you're writing, if you don't mind my asking?"

"Of course not. I'm working on an investigative piece about the Harrington disappearance. Surely you've heard about that one?"

The man smiled. "Who hasn't?"

"Well, I have evidence that tells me the whole thing began here in New Mexico's high desert. Want to have a look?" She pointed to the small computer on the table.

It didn't escape Mel's notice that the other two

had been nosing around in the kitchen and living room. One of them went down the hall and took a quick glance in each of the other rooms. He came back into the dining room, shaking his head. Thank God for Carolyn's fetish about keeping things neat and tidy, she thought.

"Nothing, Sam," the other one who had been poking around in the living room said. He sounded disappointed and almost disgusted.

"Okay, let's pack it up and get out of here. We've got a lot of territory to cover today. Sorry if we bothered you ma'am. Oh, by the way, what is your name, ma'am? Just for the record."

"Mel. Uh...Mellisa Landers. And your coming didn't bother. It was time for me to take a break anyway, before my eyes start crossing. By the way, what has this fugitive of yours done? Anything I'd like to write about?"

"I'm not allowed to discuss that, ma'am. May I see you ID plates?"

She extracted her cards and showed them to him. He nodded, and she knew anonymity for her had just evaporated.

"I...I just thought that if he was all that dangerous, I'd get my shotgun down off the wall and sleep with it by the bed. You know. Just in case he does show up."

"That wouldn't be a bad idea. Want us to check back later?"

"No...that's okay. This place is pretty far off the main trails. Not much out here anyone would want, but thanks anyway."

"That old truck out there yours?"

142

"Um—no. It was here when I rented this place."

"How do you get around, ma'am?"

"Taxi, when I need to go into town—or I rent a car when I need to go out for some distance. Why?"

"Just curious, ma'am. Have a good day," he said and ushered his two companions out ahead of him.

The door closed and Mel walked to the window. She waved good-bye as they pulled out of the drive. When they were out of sight, she turned back toward the living room and came close to collapsing. Her knees jellied and her breathing turned shallow and rapid. Damn. What next?

* * *

30 January 2054: 1800 MST

Lathrop sat down, leaned back and propped his feet up on his desk again. He smiled affably and stoked up another cigar.

"Well, Dr. Klein, after four hours of a grueling grilling under the influence of some of the most powerful drugs known, I am convinced that you are and have been telling us the truth. Your involvement in anything organized against the government is merely the result of overactive imaginations applying large slabs of paranoia to those agencies responsible for hunting you down and locking you up in our little camp. Unfortunately, all that will not get you released, but it will get the dogs off the rest of your family's

143

scent—if that is any consolation to you."

Klein nodded and smiled weakly.

Lathrop smiled back, handed Klein a carton of cigarettes from the bottom drawer of his desk, and continued.

"These are to assure that you remain in your drugged state on the off- chance any further truth emerges during the remainder of this week. I must also tell you that I enjoyed our little chat and, if you'd like, we'll have another. I have learned a lot I was not told about my job from you. I'm afraid I didn't like hearing most of it. Do you play chess, Dr. Klein?"

Outside, a cold, relentless wind howled across the yard. Klein raised his coat's collar and headed off toward his quarters. He laughed quietly. His discussion with Lathrop had covered an entire spectrum of topics, but never once touched on his family or their whereabouts. His main interests were what his work really meant, the cometary flux rate and what could be done to survive the approaching storm without going to extremes. He knew surprisingly little about the Lazarus program.

Interesting that they haven't told these people the truth, either. It's also nice to know Lathrop's not just another rotten politician. * * *

Like a caged animal, Scolini paced, hands clasped tightly behind his back. He turned with the speed of a skittish cat and jammed his nose against the nose of the agent in front of him.

"They've got to be out there somewhere, damn it. I know it. I can feel it."

"I'm sorry, sir. We've covered the entire search

area three times. There are a few civilians scattered around, but no one that remotely resembles the people we're looking for are in the sector you gave us."

"What about that writer bitch?"

"She checked out—clean. And her story matches what we got from Tampa."

"The truck?"

"Also clean. Belonged to a prospector named Andrew Greeley, but he's been dead for ten years."

"Where was he from?"

"What we got from the bureau said he was most recently from some little place east of here."

"What little place?"

Checking his notepad the officer answered, "Um...Jal, sir."

"Jal, huh? Then what the hell is that truck doing all the way over here?"

"I...don't know, sir."

"Then find out...and do it now."

Scolini whirled and moved to the group manning the machines in the op-center.

"Do we have anything more on Stone?"

"No, sir," one of them said. "Total silence from all agencies involved, and nothing has turned up in our search zone. No sign of their vehicle. Nothing."

"Get our best assault team together and send them to my quarters. I want to see them at twenty-two hundred hours. And I want the latest we have on the Stones and the Kleins sent over with them. Everything—no matter what it is—I want it all. There has to be a connection—something binding them together—and I want to know what it is.

Anything on our missing man?"

"No, sir."

* * *

30 January 2054: 2130 MST

Dyllan's voice burst from the intercom, "Hustle
your butt back out here, Wendell. You've got to see
this while it's going down."

"What's going down?"

"The program you wanted to air? Well, you've
been upstaged by a couple of days."

"You're recording it, right?"

"Of course I'm recording it, you dunderhead.
Coming or not?"

"Pipe it down here. We'll watch what we
missed later. Where's it coming from?"

"The Vatican, man. No less than the Pope
himself. He's pouring out the whole rotten mess and
not hanging back with a single punch. Should be up
on your screen now."

* * *

Scolini and his entire operations staff, mouths
agape, sat transfixed as the broadcast played out.
There was a brief, scathing, powerful presentation
by the Pope in which he laid bare the world's
governmental plans for saving the core of Earth's
infrastructure while leaving the masses in the dark.
He then informed the public that he and all the
Vatican staff were offered safe haven in some

obscure place in Africa near the equator. After that, several of the Vatican's astronomers gave the details of their observations, plus some predictions for early impacts. Then, geologists, experts in geomorphology, spelled out the implications for Earth and its environs as the planet, pummeled by comets and probably other debris that would most assuredly be knocked loose from the asteroid belt, went through its convulsions. The case for making preparations was then presented by highly respected individuals in several other disciplines. They made their points well and no government in the world had the nerve to try stopping the broadcast.

Of course. They're planning on setting up in the caverns. I'll be a son-of-a.... That's the string that holds them together. The damned caves. They think they'll be safe down there.

* * *

Before the end of the Vatican's shocking presentation, Mexican troops were massing at their northern border, preparing to repel an expected civilian invasion from the north.

One Mexican general was heard to remark, "We owe thanks to our neighbors in the north for having built such a wonderful wall and fine fences to keep the wet-backs out, no?"

All border crossings were closed down within minutes of the end of the Pope's program and convoys of more soldiers were wending their way north from points in central Mexico.

The Great Comet War between the U.S. and

Mexico officially began when one of the Mexican Border Patrol helicopters was brought down by small arms fire while on a routine flight along the frontier near Matamoros on 30 January 2054 at 2345 CST. The president of Mexico declared a state of war existed as of that time. There was no official government response from the U.S. other than to deny any involvement in the action. All the skirmishes remained limited to Mexican troops and U.S. civilians trying to cross the border to go south.

Reports of similar occurrences in other parts of the world soon rolled in and it appeared that the border conflicts were going to turn nasty and global in a big hurry.

The U.S. agreed with Mexican demands not to interfere with the unrest at the border and said flatly that no federal troops would be moved to the frontier in exchange for free overflight permission from the Mexican government. Transports carrying key people to their southern hideouts now had access to Mexican airspace with Mexican Air Force escorts to make sure no Yankee shenanigans were tried in the process. None of that news was made public.

* * *

"All right, Scolini, what do we do now?" one of the agents asked. "We're going to do what we were hired and trained to do. That's what."

"Did you see the same broadcast I did? We've all been conned, man. They were going to leave us here with snow and ice climbing up to our butts

148

while they sipped martinis in Peru and Chile. I, for one, am outa here. See you in the southland."

The agent turned and started for the door. Scolini raised his pistol and shot him in the head. He took a quick look around the room. No one moved.

"Until we're ordered to do differently, we'll do as we've been told.

Anyone else with the bright idea of leaving here or deserting their post will be...eliminated. Now, make connection with our assault team and check on their progress. Somebody...get that asshole out of here...and clean up this mess."

* * *

30 January 2045: 2300 MST

A caustic alarm sounded at the same time the first shot came through a window and lodged in the living room wall with a resounding thwack! It narrowly missed little Jason Hathaway who was jumping on the sofa against the wall. Roberta and Carolyn grabbed the screaming children and pushed them to the floor. Dyllan Drake yanked open a closet in the hall, pulled down a false ceiling and began tossing weapons into the living room. The house turned into a shooting gallery.

"Stay behind the walls," Dyllan shouted. "They're lined with armor and, unless they've brought some artillery with them, you'll be safe there."

"I guess they didn't see the Pope's broadcast,"

149

Wendell said as he picked up one of the rifles and stepped through glass shards to a shattered window.

Dyllan moved a picture hanging on the front wall. He pressed a button hidden behind it and shutters closed over all the windows. The only openings remaining were small gun ports in the shutters. "Now we don't have to worry about gas, grenades, and H.E. rounds. Those creeps are in for one helluva surprise as soon as they cross the Drake Line."

"Drake Line?" Wendell said.

"You taught me this one. Never set up anywhere without a defense perimeter. Remember? Ha! Looks like my paranoia is going to pay off. I got a couple hundred smart mines around the house. Double that around the barn. They were armed when I closed the shutters. Yes, sir, one helluva surprise."

"Where the hell did you—?"

"Would you believe...war surplus?" Dyllan said with a robust laugh.

Amid the thumps! of slugs plowing into foamed ceramic tile, the distinctive burp of twin twenty-mm cannons resonated from outside.

"Can't beat that for timing. That would be one Firefly on approach," Dyllan said, laughing even louder. "Chew'em up, boy—chew'em up."

Dyllan's surveillance cameras showed five vehicles retreating down the road and several bodies lay scattered in the dirt about three hundred meters from the house. There were no more shots and there was no movement.

An H-29-T helicopter rested on the ground by

the barn, its twin, scythe-like rotors slowing silently.

* * *

31 January 2054: 0025 MST

"Sir, five of our vehicles just passed the southern checkpoint. They were headed south in a big hurry. Didn't even try to slow down—just roared right on through. Do we have anything going on south of here?"

"No. What vehicles?"

"Assault team Bravo."

"Get them on the radio—now."

His best team was going south? They couldn't have seen the broadcast, he thought. Where on this planet do they think they're going— and why?

"Bravo One," a voice boomed from the speaker.

"This is Ops-Center," Scolini said. "Where are you going...and where's Stone and his gang?"

"Where are they? Up in that damned ravine you sent us into. We got nailed by a stealth chopper. Lost eight, and we have two wounded. We've had it, Scolini. They're being watched over by active military angels and that tells me it's time to pull out of this one. No more. See you in El Paso, if you make it out of here alive. Bravo One, out."

"Get your ass back here—right now or, by God, I'll see to it you get burned for this."

Nothing. Not even static.

31 January 2054: 0640 EST

The expression on the Secretary of Internal Security was sour and his eyes were twitching. Stoker had known the SIS during his days at Westpoint. There, he had been a man of supreme confidence, but all of that was gone when his image came up on the screen and he now looked like a frightened and bitter old man.

"...and we are shutting down Operation Lazarus. I want you to contact all of your Sector Chiefs immediately. Close all the camps. Recall all field- ops people."

"All right, Rob. What do I tell them? Are they being reassigned, or dumped?"

"The majority of the key people will be given positions elsewhere. Some will be retired. Due to the unrest at both borders about half the active field agents will be placed with the FBI and Immigration or Border Patrol. The rest are going to be looking for jobs, but they will continue to receive their current pay for one year."

"That's more than fair."

"Under the circumstances...well, you know what I mean. Oh, between you, me, and the fencepost, your name is on the list. Don't let that out to anyone. You and your family are due to be ferried out in...um...June of fifty- nine. You'll be notified two weeks in advance. Take care of yourself, Abram, and I'll be seeing you in the bunker."

The screen faded and the panels closed.

How long has it been? Eighteen days? Eighteen short days of bloody hell...and it's over—just like that. A few words from the Pope and...bang! At least we're on the list. Thank God for that, anyway.

Stoker poured out a large glass of cognac and settled into his easy chair. He was going to get fuzzy drunk, only this time it was for a different reason.

153

Chapter 9

Winding Down to a Beginning 5 February 2054: 1050 MST

"We have a slight problem, Emery," Fred Lathrop said, pacing the length of his office like a cougar in a cage.

"Oh?"

"We've all been recalled and Lazarus has been buried deep...where it damn well belongs."

"And how could that possibly pose a problem?"

"The guards all flew out of here before the official notice came in, probably because of the Pope's little program, but they left everything locked up and the towers active. We couldn't leave here if we wanted to."

"That's a problem, all right. What do we do?"

"I don't...know. All the power for the compound is outside the fence. I thought about shorting out the system but that would only affect us. The towers and security systems are on separate circuits and external power supplies."

"That is a problem. I don't suppose there's any kind of computer link to—"

"I'm afraid not. They thought of everything. I tried calling for help, but all the units that we had access to are down. Seems no one could wait to get out of this mess, and the transceiver we have here is tuned to specific frequencies in the ISA net. Is there anyone in our group savvy enough to change the frequencies in the radio?"

"Yeah, but that wouldn't do any good. Line of

sight transmission and the antenna tower is outside the fence line. As you said, 'They thought of everything.'"

"We have enough supplies to feed our little group for six weeks, after that...?"

"Do we have a regular supply schedule?"

"We had a regular schedule, before all this. Now? I can't say."

"Tunnel our way out?"

"The whole area is planted with sensors that feed directly to the gun towers. No way."

"Do you want to play another game of chess, Fred?"

* * *

When they arrived, they found the doors locked, windows scraped clean and blinds down. In the lower right corner of the window to the main entrance a small note, hurriedly written, contained a 1-800 number and a note that read "...call this number for further information on status and allotments."

Scolini cursed while he punched in the number on his wrist pad. The men behind him pressed in as if they might be able to hear what was going to be said on the phone.

"Scolini, Marvin G. N two-one-four-six K. El Paso office.... Um, there are eighteen of us, sir."

After a brief time, he popped the phone button from his ear, muttered a string of profanities and looked at the men around him. His face flushed red and his expression screamed out an anger born of frustration that no one could miss.

"The sons-of-bitches couldn't wait to get out of here and leave us with our butts swinging free. We're supposed to report to the local office of Internal Security for further instructions."

They shouldered their way through a steady, slow moving parade of dour-faced people, some of them pushing overloaded shopping carts, many of them armed and grim. All were headed south toward a ball of traffic that had packed to a standstill in the choked streets. There was no sign of a police presence anywhere. At the curb, Scolini and his gang climbed into unmarked black vans, made a quick u-turn and headed north for Montana Avenue. The sound of gunfire erupted behind them. He cast a smirking glance at the listless, southerly drift of people and said, "I wonder where the hell they think they're going? The Mexes won't let'em cross."

Welcome to the old west, he thought.

* * *

5 February 2054: 1110 MST

Chess pieces flew, scattering across the floor. Windows blew in around the compound and buildings shook as the shockwaves of three nearly simultaneous blasts traveled across the grounds. Lathrop went to the wax- slicked linoleum surface, helpless as a dry leaf in a tornado. A long, sharp spear of glass pierced his right shoulder. Klein and his chair were tossed backward and came to an abrupt halt against the far wall with enough force to take all the air out of his lungs.

Out on the once fenced-in grounds, the sally port and two northern towers were reduced to jagged teeth of broken concrete and spiny fingers of twisted steel. Fences, rolled up in haphazard balls of wire and twisted metal posts, lay strewn across the flat, white sand.

"What the hell was that, Rob—the prelude to Armageddon?"

"Good God Almighty," Dyllan chimed in.

"Hey, I'm just a pilot, not an ordnance man. We loaded whatever we could find that would fit the hard points on this bird. If I had known you—"

"Forget it, Rob. Forget it. It's okay. They did what we needed to do,cright? Now, do you suppose you could swing out far enough to get the southwest tower...only this time with a little more finesse?"

"Finesse coming up," Stahl said and slewed the Firefly out enough to see the tower. There was a brief, guttural belch from the underslung pods that pummeled the tower's top into fine powder. "Was that better?" Stahl said. He was smiling one of those smiles that let people know the smiler is feeling a certain, rather grand pride of accomplishment.

"Much better. Now, set us down so we can see if anyone survived your first gentle stroke."

"Um...you're not a little curious about why no one's here?"

"We picked up heat signatures from the buildings. They're here."

"The guests, maybe, but no guards. If I'd been in the tower I justcpulverized I'd have anticipated that last move and had a couple of lasers ready the

157

instant our ugly nose came out of hiding. No guards, man."

* * *

5 February 2054: 1230 MST

"Where are they? They should be here by now," Sandra Klein said from the couch where she sat with her knees folded close to her chest.

Worry dripped from her forehead and found its way into her reddened eyes. She blinked it away and went back to biting at her nails and rocking slowly from side to side.

"Don't fret so much, my dear," Lolly said. "Dyllan and Wendell are both trained and experienced men in these things. Trust me, they'll get your man back—safe and sound—you'll see."

The words sounded good, but they were only words. So much could go wrong. Her mind was racing, chasing after its tail in a deepening negative rut and she couldn't stop.

What if their information was wrong? Were they sure they had the right camp? And what about all the guards? Soldiers? Could they even get close enough to extract my Em from that dreadful place?

Stop, stop, stop, she thought. Can't stop. I...need my Em. I want— Mel's voice interrupted her mental flagellation.

"Sandy. Sandy...look—the helicopter is coming down by the barn. I think it's—"

Sandra Klein was off the couch and out the door before Mel could finish, pumping her long legs up the short hundred meters to the building on the hillock behind the house where the Firefly was hovering in a swirling cloud of grit. An Olympic sprinter couldn't have done better. Her heart pounded out a quickening out-of-synch rhythm as she neared the artificial whirlwind. Everyone from the house followed her up the incline.

The side door slid back. Emery Klein stepped off the machine first and all her energy drained in an instant. Sandra Klein knew she was going to faint on the run. Oh, damn it, she thought. Then she crumpled and hit the ground hard. Her world spun around her and vision tunneled, dimmed, went black. Flashes of brilliant colors and bright, white spots swam in the darkness. Someone scooped her up in strong arms. She heard what sounded like Emery's voice whispering, but she couldn't respond. After that, there was nothing.

* * *

"...and you will report for retraining Monday at 0800."

"What? What if I don't want to be in the Border Patrol?"

"Look, we have no handy options other than to relieve you of duty from the ISA. You'll receive full pay over the period of one year if we do that. Then you'll be on your own. I have to tell you, though, that with what's happening now, any kind of work is going to be harder and harder to find over the next few years, money will be worth less and less and things are in for a big shake up at all levels. All

159

of that is going to happen sooner than later. Take it or leave it, Mr. Scolini. This is your last chance."

"What the hell is the Border Patrol needing people for? There's no traffic coming this way as far as I could tell."

"They're policing the border to try stopping little gunfights here and there. From your record, you should fit right in."

"What are you trying to say—my record?"

"They have orders to shoot anyone firing weapons in any direction, Scolini."

"Okay. So, what happens if I take it?"

"You'll be guaranteed work right up to sixty-one."

"To sixty-one. After that, what?"

"After that, the federal government officially ceases to exist, if the bastards don't duck out before then—and I wouldn't put that past them. Then, you'll have to take care of yourself. I'd suggest you get ready for the inevitable. Take the job."

* * *

9 February 2054: 1200 MST

The reporter giving the daily news tried valiantly to hide her emotions but it didn't work. Facial muscles twitched, blinks were unevenly spaced and too frequent, and the perspiration beading on her forehead glistened in the camera lights. She was...nervous and distraught.

"...we have just been given shocking news that all major stock exchanges will be closing their doors—permanently—at the bell on Friday. Worldwide economies are collapsing with the news of that closure. A run on banks around the globe started early this morning after a representative from the International Monetary Exchange leaked the news of the impending market closure to several network executives around the world.

"The effects of this news and the Papal broadcast have been devastating. Everything is being reduced to shambles and there remains six and a half years to the first predicted meteor strike. A prediction, by the way, that has not been verified by anyone in the responsible scientific community. There has been a strange silence from that side and this reporter is suspicious that."

"Vid off," Dyllan said. "Well, Wendell, everything's falling a-fucking- part. Exactly what you wanted, but what do we do now—jump off the cliff with the rest of the lemmings?"

"We bide our time. We'll have a better picture of what's happening in a few days and then we can start working on rebuilding the caverns. We can't afford to wait too long, though, or we'll end up cutting our own throats."

"Somehow I find that to be a disturbing thought," Mel said. "Those caverns have been here a lot longer than we have been wandering on Earth—hell, longer than even the earliest hominids. Now we're going in to remodel them? Go right in there and create a habitat for frightened animals. How egocentric of us. And the bats? What do we do about the bats?"

"To hell with the bats," Daniel Klein said.

"And we're not frightened animals. More like a species trying to save itself. As for those damned winged rats, we wall'em in...they die. We toss'em out...they die. We leave a hole big enough for the little beasties to come and go...they die, and we do, too...more than likely."

"Dan's right, Mel," Emery Klein said. "The average surface temperature is going to drop more than twenty degrees within a couple of months after enough of the big impactors hit, depending upon how big they are and how much volcanic activity they stir up. Life's pretty fragile when environmental changes that drastic occur in a short time. Food for the bats will begin disappearing fast...and we can't risk anyone being bitten by starving, rabid bats."

"We must also not forget that people who have not thought seriously about their survival will be trying to get in—by whatever means—around the middle of sixty, if not before," Fred Lathrop said, his voice steady and calm. "A lot of people will think of the caverns by then, and the 'clan' must be kept to a specific level for us to survive in and with what we have available. Our two geneticists have determined we can remain healthy enough as a group for a few generations if that number is about a thousand but, more importantly, we will not have enough room or sustainable energy resources in there for the gardens and livestock we'll need to feed a community much larger than that. We will probably devise more efficient means in the future, but in the meantime, that is the way it is. I think it won't be long before we are forced to physically fend off a lot of people, if we are not walled up and ready soon. No more than three or four years, I would say. And...it can only get worse from there."

"We also need to look at some radical changes in our social mores if we expect to survive as a community," Sandra Klein added. "Older members will have some difficulty with that, I know, but we can begin conditioning the young ones early."

"I can guess what that means," Mel said. A half-smile graced her face and a small chuckle escaped, but concern filled her coffee-with-cream eyes.

* * *

22 February 2054: 2200 MST

A brilliant, full moon neared transit in a cloudless dark sky, scattering silver and black patches across the brush covered desert and Monday was coming fast. Two days of freedom from long nights squeezed into the blind approached.

Things inanimate took on odd forms and seemed to move. Scolini raised the night scope to his eye and made another sweep of his area. A group of six men were crawling southeasterly across his field of vision, all of them armed. He tapped his half-sleeping partner on the shoulder.

"Huh? What?"

"Shut up," Scolini growled out in a low whisper. He raised two fingers to his eyes and pointed in the direction of the movement with his other hand. Fully awake now, his associate raised his scope and turned it in the direction indicated by Scolini's rigid finger.

"Damn it, Marvin. Not now. Our weekend is coming up. Why don't we let this one slide and hand it off to the graveyard shift?" he said, keeping his voice low.

"They won't be here for two hours, man."

"So? We just stay quiet and let them move on to wherever they think they're going. They won't get far before the Mexicans nail'em anyway and save us the trouble, not to mention the serious chance of getting frikkin' shot and spoiling our weekend."

"Standing order of the day. We stop anyone armed, take them into custody so that Mexican thing doesn't happen. They say it's bad for international relations."

"What international relations would those be? There are no international relations now, far as I can tell...and what if they put up a fight? There are six of them and, if my arithmetic is right, that makes it three to one."

"If they resist...well-l-l, you know, all the stops get pulled. And we're not going to get shot—but they might."

"Who do you think you are...Superdoop or something?"

"Or something. We have our orders. We follow them." With that, Scolini rose from the blind and flipped on the huge floods that shone like a low sun, sending shadow fingers into infinity and bathing the six crawlers in glaring light. He raised the bullhorn to his mouth and took two large caliber slugs square

164

in the chest. A third ripped through his thigh. He reeled and fell back into the blind with no air in his lungs and oozing blood from the wound in his leg. The oozing was good, at least nothing critical had been torn apart. He looked at his partner, blank white with a neat little hole above his right eyebrow. Everything faded and the only thing Scolini was aware of at all was a constant humming sound in his head louder than a Mormon choir warming up.

* * *

2 March 2054: 0900 MST

Stone stared at the preliminary drawings on the screen. The drawings, prepared by two physicists-turned-engineers, showed a low domed structure covering the natural opening to the caverns. That structure, they said, would provide the strongest, most material conservative cap for the entrance, considering its size. He didn't doubt their word, but it looked to be a supremely difficult thing to construct with the few people they now had in their yet to be formed colony. "What do you think, Dyllan?"

"I think it's a good example of why we have physicists and engineers.

Physicists are good at physics, and engineers are good at engineering. In other words, I think we need to find an engineer willing to join us."

"Yeah. I think you're right—but it is a start."

"Uh-huh. Such as it is. I'm going over to the

big city this afternoon for some stuff we need. Want me to see if I can scrounge up a real engineer? Um...that is, if anyone's left over there."

"That bad?"

"Yeah, from what I hear. And the stores are all but empty."

"How about our lovebirds? Have they come down from their tower of passion?"

"Jeremy didn't tell you?"

"I haven't seen Jeremy in over two weeks, except when he comes in for his food handouts and he's too busy stuffing his mouth to say much."

"Both of the Kleins are helping him with the polishing of that mirror. Oh, and they say that they're going to have to silver it. Seems they can't find anyone still in business to do the aluminizing, and the shipping and delivery services have all gone all four to the sky, too. The stuff they need they say they can get from the university in Las Cruces or El Paso when the time comes."

"Things are coming unglued too fast, damn it."

"That they are."

* * *

2 March 2054: 1230 EST

Stoker threw a chair across his private den at the open panel with its gawking screens. It did no good. The monitors were covered in bullet proof material. The chair just bounced off and landed perilously close to his feet. He was as drunk as anyone could get without passing out and angry enough that he knew he needed to remain in his private domain until he calmed down or he would kill the first person he saw. Probably his wife or his aide.

Shit. Nothing's going right and no one's telling it straight. I have to find someone in charge who will be decent enough to tell me the truth, instead of trying to feed me so much BS.

The combox burped out its signal. "Yeah?"

"DoD incoming, sir. D.C."

"Put'em through. Comp, seal the room."

Stoker recognized the face that materialized on the screen. General Clive Tamps, four stars and a fire-breathing dragon's personality...with breath to match. He looked...unhappy.

"Afternoon, Clive. How goes the battle out your way?"

"Downhill, and damned fast. You look like you're doing the same thing. Did you get the news about them ferrying the pres out last night?"

"No, I didn't. No one's telling me anything. What does that signify for us?"

"Not much. Our darling said she's still in charge and in touch with all that's going on and that she's just operating from her bunker in whatever stinking South American hell-hole of a cave they've stuck her in. It seems there's some serious talk of revolution and they moved her out early...just in case."

"Bullshit."

"No doubt. Looking beyond that, we are in the process of relocating a lot of our personnel and you were high on the list."

"Uh-oh. What kind of relocation are we talking about?"

"You have your choice of three. Benning, Biggs AAF, or Bragg. If I were in your shoes, I'd take the Biggs deal. Probably the best you can do to get away from all this and still be near the fibrillating heart of America...and all the transports that are going to fly south when the time comes. Plus, you'll be able to watch the fun at the border down there. I understand it's heating up to a full blown shooting war between trained Mexican troops and disgruntled gringos trying to push their way across the border. According to what I've heard, my money's on the gringos—better armed and equipped, you know. Some of them have more combat experience than both of us put together."

* * *

2 March 2054: 1110 MST

An angel drifted by. All covered over in white and shimmering in a stark light coming from somewhere overhead. He tried to move and found he couldn't. He felt restrained, leaden, and weak. There was a dull touch of pain coming from somewhere but he couldn't determine where. His eyes opened a bit more and the angel morphed into a youngish nurse—blond with glowing pink cheeks and the slightest hint of freckles. The sort one always hopes to find at their bedside but usually winds up face to face with a three hundred pound matron gorilla wearing an evil grin, knee-high white

168

stockings slightly rolled down and latex gloves.

"Ah...nice to see you've awakened, Mr. Scolini. How are you feeling?" He mumbled incoherently.

"Don't try too hard. Not yet. I'll bet that throat of yours is really dry, huh? We just took the tubes out an hour ago, so that's normal. You just let me get my special little bottle and we'll see if we can fix that for you. Okay?"

He mumbled again and she clicked her tongue at him in mock scold. She left the room and returned what seemed to him an eternity later with a small plastic bottle filled with something pale blue. She leaned down over him.

"Okay. Open up and we'll get your throat all smooth again."

He let his jaw fall and she sprayed what tasted vaguely like cranberries and mint into his mouth and down into his throat. The difference was instant—and miraculous.

"What...what is that stuff?" he croaked.

"Oh, now, don't you worry yourself about that, hon. You wouldn't be able to pronounce it anyway. It works. That's what counts. Isn't that right, now?"

Scolini thought her distinct Texas drawl was pleasant—comforting. "How long?"

"How long what, sweety? Oh, I know. You want to know how long you've been out. Well, let me see."

She punched a couple of keys on the wall.

"Probably about six and a half days. You all had yourself quite a time out there. You've got two cracked ribs and that shot to your leg clipped the femur and knocked your hip out of kilter."

"Six and a—"

"Sh-h-h. I told you not to overdo it. My secret mixture is good, but it doesn't work if you insist on breaking the rules. Now, hush up."

"Where—?"

"Well, now, there you go again. Just can't seem to follow orders, can you?" She giggled and it was a musical wind-chime on the zephyr breeze smelling of a touch of delicate perfume from her smock passing by his face. "For your information, you're in the Fort Bliss infirmary. According to what I see on your chart, you're going to be here for a couple of months before they put you back into the workforce, so you'll have plenty of time to find out all you want to know. You're also going to have some trouble with your hip for a while—long time before you'll be running track again. That means, relax, hon. Now, let me give you one more little squirt of Mattie's Magic Elixir, then I'm going to leave so you're not tempted to ruin all the good we've done."

* * *

18 March 2054: 1700 MST

The Federal News Network, the only one still running on a regular basis, came on and everyone in the house, now numbering thirty-four, gathered around the screen to hear the latest "official news" from the government. The reporter's face was somber as he began reading the teleprompter without so much as a pretense at looking natural.

"The National Guard has been redeployed to help run farms throughout the country and all food processing plants have been federalized to keep them running. There is no need to—"

"Ha! That's a good one," Daniel Klein said. "Now it's the National Gardener and the National Grocer. What's next?"

"...and they are concentrating on producing freeze-dried products that will last through the predicted extended winter and acidic rains that will deplete the nation's food supplies to low levels."

"Extended winter? And 'deplete,' my ass," he inserted. "More like 'delete,' I'd say. Why can't they tell us anything the way it is?"

"Because they don't want to panic an already nervous public that's on the verge of going insane," Mel said. "Think of what it would be like if everyone out there knew the whole truth about what will be happening to them soon. The Pope even tried to downplay most of the more gory details because he knew what the result would be. Chaos— total anarchy. The government has been careful not to touch much on the truth in any of the areas of survival. It's already bad enough out there and the economies of the world have gone to hell at just the casual mention of an impending global disaster. All the businesses that were in the old town of Carlsbad are gone—no one is here but us."

The reporter droned on. Nobody paid any attention.

"That's enough of that. Vid...off." Stone positioned himself in front of the darkened screen on the wall. "Dan, round up all the Travelers you

171

can find in the area. Especially those with any construction or heavy equipment experience. Jeremy, how close are you to finishing that mirror?"

"Two days...tops, dad. We'll be ready to silver it in four. Everything else is ready to assemble and mount as soon as we have a building up there to house it."

"Great. I need a couple of volunteers to go down to the caverns first thing tomorrow morning to see what's happening there."

Lathrop and one of the younger ex-prisoners from Camp 32 stepped forward.

* * *

30 March 2054: 2100 MST

A waning half moon hung low in the sky, its silver light dulled occasionally by the shoulders of high, cumulus clouds stacking up on the western slope of the Guadalupe Mountains. The build up that threatened rain before sunrise was a joke in New Mexico for as many years as anyone cared to remember. Maybe...maybe not. The best meteorological predictions for the area and the plains to the east were those made by sticking your head out a window once in a while and looking around.

Wendell surveyed the mound of materials and collection of equipment huddled around the natural opening to the caverns. It seemed to be a lot of stuff, but it was just a beginning to a large, time consuming project.

172

All the stalactites would have to come down and stalagmites leveled.

They would then be crushed and used as the base for the plazas and gardens to be laid through the center of the new cavern floors. Most of the more substantial columns would be left in place. Hard gravel, thousands of cubic meters of it, would be brought in to cover the base to a depth of nearly a meter, followed by another meter or so of ordinary dirt and an equal amount of topsoil and growing mix. There was plenty of guano in the caverns to bring up the nitrogen, phosphorous and potassium content to near the desired level, the rest would be supplied by a huge and vacant home and farm supply warehouse east of the new city.

The new city, itself, was largely deserted and most of the stores had been left unattended but intact—shelves stocked with a dwindling supply. The folks who had remained, a mere handful, wandered in whenever they felt like it and helped themselves. The same held true for the grand mall in the center of the city; empty and dark as the caverns, but still up and running for anyone who needed something. It wouldn't be long before someone tumbled to the fact that there would be no deliveries for restocking them—the hoarding would begin. The colony would get there first. Stone would see to that. Tomorrow? Probably.

Electricity was still being fed to the city from the automated grid, but it was anybody's guess as to how long that would continue before something broke down. With no one there to maintain the plants, it was no more than a matter of time. The large nuclear plants installed at the park two years ago and located at the eastern end of the visitors' center at the top of the caverns would supply most of the power needed to run their systems for at least a century, if they were frugal and reserved the energy available for the gardens and small hospital where it would be needed most. Those units would be moved inside the security perimeter so they couldn't be plundered or rendered inoperable by anyone. They would use energy from the grid as long as it was there, then revert to the park's nukes, holding Stone's small units in reserve for hospital emergencies only. The basic infrastructure for the colony was being handed to them without so much as a grunt of resistance. He smiled at that thought and laughed out loud.

Where in hell did all those people out there think they were going? he wondered. It won't be much warmer in the south, not so much that you would notice it, anyway—and in some ways it would be worse for storms in the radically changing weather fronts. Gigantic storms that could flare up in minutes, according to what the Kleins and some of their colleagues had to say. He pointed the beam of his flashlight down into the gaping mouth of the cavern entry and it swallowed the light as fast as a black hole gobbles stars. He shuddered at the thought of the amount of work facing them. It was...intimidating.

"It's a nice night for thinking, isn't it?" she said from somewhere behind him.

"What are you doing out here, Mel?"

"Same as you...I think. I couldn't sleep, so I

174

wandered out here for a look and a think or two."
She moved up beside him. "We have a long way to
go, don't we?"

"A long, long way, Mel. A long, long way."

Chapter 10

It had been a blistering hot summer but was giving way to more agreeable days and cooler nights. The last pour of high density poxycrete was being troweled out on the "properly engineered" geodesic steel and concrete dome. Thanks to an engineer Daniel Klein had uncovered in Artesia it had gone into place without the need of skyhooks and other magic that the original drawings would have required. The attractive and graceful structure covering the natural entrance to the caverns was in its final stage. Only the gloss coat to keep the dome as clear of ice and snow as possible remained before the cap could be called complete. The security tunnels and ingress/egress chambers, rising to twelve meters above ground level, were finished the week before and stood out as gleaming white triangular extremities and attached structures.

The completion of the dome marked the final grand milestone for their project and four hundred seventy-one people gathered to celebrate the occasion. Sure, there remained myriad details to take care of, but the dome was the last of the major projects.

No one could actually place a date on when it happened but, a couple of months before this event, the power coming in from the grid stopped with surprising abruptness, as if someone had yanked the plug from its socket.

Shortly after that, the new city of Carlsbad had

ceased to exist as a place of habitation and was transformed into nothing more than hollow shells of glass, steel, and concrete, standing vacant, silent—forlorn in the desert heat, picked as clean of their contents as the bones of a thirsty, careless steer at the Amazon's edge that had fallen prey to ravenous piranhas. Homes that once held families living out their lives in what they thought would last forever served as nothing more than elegant, already erected tents to shelter wanderers coming through from the east and the north for a short time while they gathered the strength they needed to continue their trek to an unforeseeable future.

Little traffic moved on the highways except members of the "clan" in their trucks and the occasional group of cyclists traveling south, overstuffed packs wobbling rhythmically and precariously on their sweating backs.

Some had little trailers, tagging obediently along behind, loaded with children or more of their personal possessions—often both. There were small clusters who walked. A few striding, the rest struggling. None appeared to take notice of the activity atop the bluff to their west.

Since the power from the grid was off, no one without portable generating units could travel in their cars at all, except near major cities where power was still available from the grid. There were no charging stalls to re-energize their systems and their small solar panels were only able to keep a minimum system charge for the onboard computers, communication, and location equipment.

Fred Lathrop, standing on a podium erected at

the edge of the dome, tapped his mic and a loud thump thump thump rumbled over the crowd.

"Friends. Members of the Cave Clan, as we have come to call ourselves, we are gathered here to celebrate the last bold strokes on our canvas. A work that has included the sweat and blood of every one of us and several more who are still out gathering up some final bits and pieces from here and there.

"But, before I launch into my formal song and dance, I need to announce that nominations for the Council of Twelve will be opened on Monday, the twenty-second of September, and will continue through Friday, the twenty-sixth. Voting for the Council will be held on the third of October. For those nominated, you won't have much time for campaigning, so get out there and do your best in what time you have. "Now, for the ceremony of the day. As you can see behind me, the finishing touches are being applied to the dome. That work will be completed today. After it is finished, we will be free to begin moving in to take up housekeeping inside, but I suggest you continue living wherever you are now until the closing date. Take advantage of the world we have while we still have it. We will remain open for new arrivals until June first, 2060.

"You may be asking yourself, 'Why a year early?' and the answer to that question is simple. Our astronomy staff says that we can expect small chunks to precede the bigger ones. Some of them will be large enough to make it to the ground and do some local damage. What sort of threat that poses is unknown, so we are not going to take any chances.

We will be secured and ready for the potential danger, regardless of how small it may be. Therefore, on June first of next year we will seal all access and become real cave dwellers until it is safe enough to venture out into a cold and battered world. We, you and I, will not be there, but our descendants will be faced with it. We wish them our best.

"They will be emerging into a different place from what it is today. Our science folks have been reluctant to predict what they will find when they leave the caverns, but they are sure it will not be anything at all like it is now.

"We have grown from a scant few, running and hiding like criminals from the ISA a little over five years ago—a sad Chapter In Our History—To A Community Of Almost Six Hundred. A special thank you is owed to our Traveler friends who have...appropriated much of what we needed to convert this dream of ours from daunting fantasy to sparkling reality. That they were not able to find enough of the bubbly to toast this magnificent occasion pales when I unveil this," he said, and, with a flourish, Lathrop lifted a blue tarp from a mountain of ice cold beer and sodas on the podium behind him. "A gang of Travelers delivered a truck loaded with these goodies early this morning, so we will have our toast, anyway. Come on up folks and take your pick."

* * *

7 September 2059: 1650 MST

179

Scolini wandered out from behind a hangar and watched another giant C-95 begin its lumbering roll down the runway, its ten engines thundering.

Adding to the ruckus, the rocket assist exploded to life about halfway down the strip and everything in the area shook and rattled in response. Still, with all that applied power, it took almost every meter of the fifty-five hundred meters of picture perfect PEM surface and part of the "21 overrun" before it had reached a speed great enough to rotate and lift off. There was literally no surface left when the trailing wheels took air between them and the ground. He smiled as an image passed through his mind of gooney birds taking off from a small pond scummed over with thin, wet ice. Even without the rockets on their butts, the birds did better than the C-95 with its maxed out payload of fuel, materials, equipment and people.

The largest aircraft in the world, its long wings curved severely upward with the strain of holding their load in the air, banked to a shallow climbing left turn and vanished slowly into a low, ominous looking deck of dark clouds to the south. He was more certain than ever that the idle talk around his security sector was passing from the chatter of the ignorant and unknowing to a brutal reality.

Flights, like the one that had just departed, had been getting more frequent over the two years he had been employed as a guard at Biggs Field and the number of them that returned diminished month after month. He turned and counted those remaining on the heavies pads in the tarmac.

Twelve. Twelve more and that would be it.

Gun battles along the border continued to break out. A two mile deep, almost unbroken line of armed camps pressed up against the frontier from Tijuana in the west to Matamoros in the southeast.

From what Mattie told him, Bliss was bleeding off high placed personnel like a class one hemorrhage and, once Biggs shut down, there would be nowhere for them to go. They were going to be trapped between the crazies in the south and the nothingness he was sure existed in the north— nowhere for them to go unless those lunatics breached the Mexican line...soon. El Paso was still breathing and the local grid was still up, but who could say how long that would last?

The siren wailed and his shift was over. He stuffed his hands in his pockets and shuffled off in a limping gate to the hangar where a dark green time-clock crouched against a wall, waiting to bite his card. An anachronistic piece of third world technology hanging on one of the walls of the most advanced military installation on the planet. The sound of it grew louder in his ear each time he slipped his card into the slot. Bang! You're in. Bang!

You're out. But it was food on the table, wine in the fridge, and clothes on their backs. Bang!

Mattie had her job at Fort Bliss and he was still actively assigned to his post at Biggs, so they had access to the commissary where the prices were in the stratosphere, but lower than anywhere else. All of that was coming to an end. He knew it. When, he couldn't say. Where would they go? What would they do? Of one thing he was quite certain, they would not join the insanity at the line. The time had come to start planning their way out— their escape from the approaching disaster, as if what was going on around them wasn't already a major muddle worthy of a spot in a book of world records, if books were still being produced.

* * *

17 September 2059: 0800 MST

The fellow seated at the desk was one of those intense types. Stoker focused on the four stars on his shoulders and wondered how such a nervous little man ever made it that far. He reminded Stoker of a cross between the psychological portrait that had been painted of Napoleon years ago and a hungry rat. An insecure little man with a complex that needed tending every minute of the day. And what the little general had just told him turned in his gut. He was being deserted by the very government he had sworn to defend and he didn't like it at all. It had nothing to do with politics. It had everything to do with what seemed to him to have been several years of misplaced loyalty.

"Listen, Stoker, we all have our orders," the midget who would be emperor said. "You have been dropped from the list of advanced evac and that is the way it is. You are to take command of the Southwest Damage Assessment Unit until December, 2063...or until things get too hairy to hang on. Then, and only then, will you go south

182

with the last flight out. Understood?"

"Understood."

"Good. A situation doc will be transferred to your system in a couple of weeks. A lot of it is for your eyes only, so you will have to boil it down for the pilots and crews when they get here. We want data we can't get off the sats, and this is the only way we can get it. Fifteen long range choppers, four fixed wing surveillance aircraft and two tankers will be arriving in six weeks. They will be placed under your direct command."

Stoker knew better than to argue. It would get him nowhere. Still, there were some things that had not been said and he desperately wanted to hear them.

"What about my wife? My kids and grandchildren?"

"They are still on the list and will be ferried out early. Does that make you feel any better?"

"Yes, it does, but I still don't like the idea of being left up here like that. What happens if the last plane is wiped out during my stay? Then what? You know the Mexican government is not going to allow anyone to cross their border and there are all those other podunk countries in Central America to contend with. What about them?"

"If the last plane is destroyed you will have much, much bigger problems to concern yourself with than crossing the border, Stoker. That plane will be sitting on the tarmac...here...at Biggs...and you will be sitting here, too. See what I'm saying? But, arrangements have been made and you will be allowed across at the Zaragosa crossing, if it comes to that. All the podunks, as you called them, have signed on, too. You'll have safe passage all the way to your destination in Piura, Peru. Once there, you'll be picked up and taken to the refuge site near Tarapoto. See? It's all been mapped out. Nothing to worry about."

"Shit. Nothing to worry about, my ass."

"Okay. I understated it a little—but it has been worked out."

"You can't land these planes wherever you want. Where the hell are they going?"

"That has been one of the few secrets they have been able to keep. A long time ago, back when blocs were worth something—remember that?— we made a deal with Colombia. That's where they are going. Where in Columbia? I have no idea. They managed to keep that a secret from even me. For sure, somewhere with a long airstrip. A place the satellites consistently miss."

* * *

Stoker walked with a slow and deliberate stride. He wanted time to think. Time to digest the unpalatable meal he had just been fed by Napoleon's twin. He had been a military man all his life. His father and his father's father had been career Army, too. For Abram Stoker, orders were handed down from an unseen god seated in a high place somewhere, and it was his duty—a sworn pledge he had made in his hazy past—to follow them. No matter what. But this...this was stretching his bonds to the chain near the breaking point.

The enemy in this case was something against which there was no defense. They couldn't be stopped. They couldn't be placated into aborting their mission. And they sure as hell couldn't be wished away. You would watch the incoming and you would know there was no place to hide that was close to safe. No foxhole you could dig would protect against the missiles bullying and burning their way through the sky at close to seventy kilometers per second and exploding with the force of hundreds, perhaps thousands of megatons.

He had to think. For the first time since West Point he was torn between his duty and a nagging concern for his family and an uncertain future. "Duty, honor, country," he said out loud. He said it again, but louder—almost a shout. He repeated it several times until it took on a mantra-like quality. He stopped, looked down that long strip of runway, and took a deep breath. He shook out the stiffness in his shoulders and set a brisk pace back to his office. His thinking was done.

* * *

17 September 2059: 0920 MST

"Abram Stoker, what...what is that big thing doing in our driveway and why are you home so early?"

"That big thing, Margaret, is an APC—Heavy, and I'm home because we have several things we need to do...right away. I want you to pack our camping gear and outdoor clothes. Nothing

185

more...and call that corporal, the one who does the yard work here. Tell him to find a couple of his buddies who know how to handle an M-191 and get their tails over here...on the double. Then, call the kids on Comsat Seven and tell them to meet us at the airport in Lubbock."

"Lubbock?"

"Lubbock, Texas, dear."

"I know where Lubbock is. Why Lubbock?"

"Because it's more or less halfway between here and Tulsa. Oh, and tell them to look for an 8-wheeled personnel carrier with a trailer about the size of a small mansion. They won't be able to miss it. For all I know, it'll probably be the only vehicle out there."

"Have you been reassigned, again?"

"You can call it a reassignment, yes. Right now, I need a shower to get this stink off me. Hustle, Margaret. We don't have much time."

* * *

20 September 2059: 1920 MST

Mattie began removing the remains of dinner from the table and tossing them into the recycler while Marvin rotated his cup of lukewarm coffee. He was in a pensive and decidedly sour mood. She could see he was edgy and his worry showed in a furrowed brow and darting eyes that couldn't seem to fix on any one thing longer than a second.

"You said things are weird over there at Biggs. What do you think is happening?"

186

"I don't know what's going on, not exactly, but it's damned strange, Mattie. The big muck-a-muck of security—some general named Stover, or something like that, anyway—has gone missing and everything's screwed up. Nobody knows what to do next and the boss man hasn't been replaced yet. I get the feeling that things are about to come apart and I don't want to be around when the other shoe drops."

"What do you think we should do, hon?"

"Get the hell out of here while we still can, that's what I think. And the sooner, the better."

"Where can we go?"

"You leave that to me. The commissary is open until ten, right?"

"Uh-huh."

"And they change cashiers every four hours...with the long shift at night?"

"Yeah, but—"

"Okay. You make a run over there every few hours so you don't see the same people every time and we start stocking up on non-perishables. Canned and dried stuff. Take what you can from the infirmary, too. Know what I mean?"

"Um...yeah."

"I'll do the same over at Biggs during the day and here at night. We should have enough to hold us over for a few months—maybe a year—in about two or three months. Then we can get ourselves out from under the big bag of BS I think is going fall on us pretty soon. Okay?"

"Well sure, but—"

"No 'buts,' baby. We get it together and we go.

187

If we don't, I know we'll be stuck here with no way out...and I don't want that to happen."

There was no mistaking the stolidness in his voice. He was being as direct and cool as she had ever heard him and that bothered her. He sounded almost like he was running on autopilot.

What she envisioned was their little commuter bulging with junk and no place for them to sit. She was also two and a half months pregnant and the thought of uprooting now was sounding a little too much for her. She was frightened, but she didn't want to say so.

"How...how are we going to haul all those groceries out of here in our little eggmobile, along with all our things? Sounds to me like we'll have a whole truckload to move."

"We don't take all our stuff. Just what we need. And we won't be using the egg, either. As for how we haul it, you leave that one to me, too."

"And the baby?"

"Where we're going, I don't think that will be a problem, either. No, I'm sure it won't. Relax. Everything's going to be okay and remember, I promised I'd take care of you, right?"

"Uh-huh."

"Well, that's exactly what I intend to do."

* * *

25 September 2059: 0945 MST

Sandra Klein stepped from the semi-enclosed veranda into their apartment. It was the first time she had seen what all the construction was producing. She stood just inside the door and inspected her surroundings.

"Oh...my goodness, Em," she said after some time, "It's...it's...precious." She moved all the way in to their new home in the First Tier Garden Apartments, her head swiveling left and right to take it all in. The walls in the living room were painted a soft salmon, which made it appear larger than it was in reality. To her left was the dinette and tiny, but handy kitchen. Off the right a door stood open. Beyond was a little bedroom and attached bathroom. It was incredibly small and she knew immediately they would have some adjusting to do to live at this scale, but it was nice. Something like an expanded doll house. It was cozy. And, above all, it would be what she would be calling "home" for the rest of her life. That little thought sent a touch of a shiver through her.

All the homes were built against the walls of the cavern and rose from the floor to the vaulted ceilings in the style of the ancient Anasazi cliff dwellings. They were, in a word, beautiful, and nearly made her forget the luster of the caverns that had been irreverently jack-hammered and blasted away to make room for the housing and the central gardens and plazas on the different tiers. The great lamps overhead that served as artificial replacements for a sun shone brightly. It was an illusion that took away her breath. It couldn't have been any more perfect.

"Yeah, it is, if you don't pay any attention to the fact that we're eight stories up, and there are only two ways to get here. Climb the ladders or ride the elevator that's only going to run at three hour intervals."

"Oh, come on, Em. That's all part of the charm, and I don't mind waiting for the elevator. It's different, that's for sure, but it's not sterile like I thought it would be—and it doesn't have a meddling computer to deal with. I...I love it."

"Okay, I'll buy that. But, where am I going to find meteorites around here to study?"

"Um...outside, and soon, silly man."

"Score one for Sandy."

"When can we move in?"

"Any time you want, but I warn you, most of the systems won't go online until the day we close the doors. The natural gas line isn't completed, either. That's the last of the major projects. All of this is just for a couple of days for people to see what they're getting into. You know...like a preview and an opportunity for those who are not so certain they want to stick it out here. There are a few of them, but not many. After that, it's going to be pretty dark down here to conserve energy, except when maintenance comes through."

"Aw...now that's not fair, Em."

"Sure it is. Oh, by the by, did you happen to look at the Upper Tier central planting area on the way down on the tram?"

"No, I was a little preoccupied when we left the entry bay. What's up there?"

"No homes. They don't want to expend the energy it would take to heat them during the cold periods. But there is an orchard of sorts. We have some apple trees, pear trees, filberts, walnuts, and all sorts of wild bush berries that need freezes to do their thing. Not many, but who's to complain about even part of a fresh apple once in a while? They're going to put in an apiary, too. That'll be on the next level down. How about that? Toast with honey."

"Stings."

* * *

30 September 2059: 1115 MST

"How are we doing, Dyllan?" Stone said as he entered the Communications and Data gathering center in the Lower Gallery. He deftly dodged cables that snaked across the floor as he made his way to the communications array. It was the only installation in the caverns that was running at full capacity.

"Great. I've established connections with two hundred and nine enclaves around the world already. It never dawned on me how many caverns there are out there and that so many people would come to the same conclusions we did. Incredible. Some of them are relying on obsolete, hardened underground missile sites, though. All of those groups are small."

"Logical," Stone said. "Are we going to be able to maintain those connections?"

"As long as we don't lose any key Comsats—and our contacts don't get hit, yeah. They're all pretty well set up out there. Technically, that is. We have standard shortwave radio for backup, but that's nowhere near as reliable. When the crap in the atmosphere gets too thick, we'll be out of touch through whatever means, though. You know, if this cave thing works out, there should be a lot of survivors and a good technology base when the dust clears."

"This cave thing had better work out...or we're all dead meat," Daniel Klein said from across the room where he sat on the floor assembling a wrist thick wiring harness for the observatory's data transfer system.

"It will. Your brother told me the chances of us being hit directly are lower than winning the world lottery."

"Yeah, but he didn't tell you that somebody wins that lottery every year. He can take his statistics and stick'em."

"Got your balls in a bind today, Dan?"

"Nope. Never felt better in my life. It's only that meteorologists have never been able to predict the weather worth a damn—less being able to tell where all the raindrops are going to fall. Know what I mean?"

"He's got a point, Wendell."

"That he does. That he does," Stone sighed. "What about the seismic array."

"The last sensing device should be set today at Guadalupe Peak. They put in what they called a Lateral Event sensor, too. That's locked into the GPS so we can tell if we're headed for the Gulf of Mexico or the Pacific."

"That's a sobering thought."

"Always wanted to own some beachfront real

estate," Daniel Klein said.

Chapter 11

Stone narrowly escaped being elected to the Council of Twelve by refusing his nomination. He based his reluctance on the fact that his other duties placed high demands on his time. He didn't want to be involved in the politics and all the maneuvering that would be going on right up to Closing Day—indeed, from the election and beyond. His time, he felt, would be best spent working behind the scenes and in what he saw as more constructive endeavors. His hands were full with his self-assigned position as Director of Security and Personnel Management. A position that included screening and interviewing members of the "Clan" and newcomers for work and housing assignments. Some were easy and straightforward. Others were...not so easy. But they were things he thought were critical to the functional survival of the "Clan" over the years they would all be confined to the caverns' cramped confines—an undefined time.

In the meantime, Daniel Klein had assembled a corps of the hardier Travelers to engage in outside activities. He had laid out a plan that included hunting and gathering to supplement what he felt would be strained supplies until the gardens and livestock were adequate to the purpose of feeding just over seven hundred people. A number he said would surely grow before Closing Day. Perhaps it would increase a little even after they sealed the caverns—no one was sure. He also proposed that they would be useful in the future by establishing contact with any possible survivors around the region when it was safe enough to venture out after the bombardment subsided...and the volcanoes stopped their unwelcome belching...to build a base of good will among those they could find—so people wouldn't get shot for walking in the snow. Stone agreed. Emery and Sandra Klein, along with Jeremy, were charged with astronomical observations, analyses, and observatory maintenance as long as such activities were even marginally possible. They would also maintain communication links with other astronomers to support and confirm their data. In Stone's opinion, things were going as well as they could.

"Wendell, we have nine more out here who want to join us. What do you want me to do with them?" Lathrop's voice said from the combox. "Shall I go ahead and assign them quarters in the interim?"

"Yeah, Fred. I've got a backlog of more than a hundred already. Set them up in White's City with the rest and tell them their interviews and assignments may not happen until sometime in January. If you want, you can bring them up here for a look. Maintenance has the lights up to near full today. You know, Fred, I can't believe how complicated this is getting."

"Hah! You have never assembled your own world before, have you? Welcome to the business of society building from scratch. We had the problem of doing just that with the Martian colonies, you know."

195

A slight click from the box let Stone know that Lathrop had dropped the connection.

Society building from scratch. Hadn't thought of it in those terms.

What do you know, Wendell Stone, Lord of the Underworld.

He scribbled a note in his personal touch pad journal. "Wendell Stone = Pluto."

* * *

14 October 2059: 1300 PST

They had pulled off the highway about 0700 and were working their way up a small valley that was closing in on them as they went. The coordinates given to him were coming up. They turned west into one of the many ravines surrounding the area and in a deep, extremely narrow gorge on the east side of the Pacific Range, Stoker knew he had found what he was looking for. The position matched on his GPS and up near the head of the ravine a group of some four hundred people were camped in front of what appeared to be the entrance to a mine. It was clearly new construction accomplished by people who knew what they were doing. The entry was built in the manner of many underground military complexes, but in miniature. His communication with this group had been limited to a few sporadic contacts, but he knew them to be made up mainly of personnel from the Yuma Proving Ground and MCAS Yuma with a mix of civilians from the

196

region encompassing Yuma.

Their choice of location was perfect, Stoker thought. High enough to be out of the way of any but the worst of Tsunamis, but deep between steep, stone covered walls so that anything hitting near them would do little direct damage and only the depth of the ejecta blanket or stone rattled loose from the slope would be of real concern. Well thought out, this one. Good planning.

Stoker climbed down from the APC and approached one of the men taking a break in the shade of a house-sized boulder.

"Excuse me. Who's in charge here, sergeant?"

"Uh...Colonel Clayton is. Who's asking?" The young sergeant's gaze caught on Stoker's two stars and he sprang to attention. "Sorry, sir. You'll find him inside, sir."

"As you were, sergeant. It's too hot out here for that stuff, don't you think?"

"Uh...yes, sir. Thank you, sir."

Indeed it was. It was the middle of October but the temperature was climbing toward the thirty-five degree mark. Odd weather for this time of year, Stoker thought, but then he didn't have any experience with this part of the country. He shrugged and turned for the tunnel entrance to have a word with this Colonel Clayton.

* * *

16 October 2059: 2220 MST

Emery Klein scooted his chair closer to the

197

console and squinted at the faint images, then read the data scrolling along the right side of the screen.

"What do you make of this, Sandy?"

Sandra Klein took her attention away from the monitor where mounting data was being chewed on by the computer to peer into the input from the night's sky sweep and gasped.

"Early birds," she said. "And far, far off the ecliptic. Can you tell what they are?"

"No. Too dim to track them well. Damn. Wish we had radar."

"Well, we don't. Any estimate of size?"

"Are you kidding? I'd guess they're large enough to do some major local damage though. They're not outgassing—rocks, probably—and too low in albedo to get much of anything off of them."

"Think we should sound the alarm?"

"Not yet. These guys are still about three months out and we don't have enough data to say they'll hit. But this is the warning shot I thought we'd get. A warning shot coming in at a little over sixty-eight kilometers per second. We should send this stuff down to MacDonald to firm it up. I hope I get a chance to see them come in."

"Em."

"It's not that I want them to hit...but what an experience it would be,

huh?"

"Em."

"Okay. Okay. But it would be an ex.... What the...?"

A red light flashed insistently on the screen. Both of them stood abruptly and looked at one another. Emery's usually smooth brow furrowed deeply.

"Ring the bell and toot the whistle, Sandy."

* * *

16 October 2059: 1150 MST

Stone sat, wringing his hands and staring intently at the empty space between the Kleins.

"Are you sure about this?" he said.

"As certain as we can be with the equipment we have, and I'm pretty confident in the data we've obtained," Emery Klein responded.

"Any prediction as to where and when?"

"Not yet. It's being...worked on. MacDonald Observatory in Texas is back in business and we sent them what ephemerides we were able to collect so they can take a look. They'll check and refine our information and get back to us in a day or so."

"How many of them are there, and do you have a tentative guess as to when they'll hit...if they do?"

"There are five that we could see. That doesn't mean there aren't more that we couldn't see. Impact? I'd say on the twelfth of January, but I really am guessing. About twenty-one hundred hours local, give or take a couple of hours if my guess is close to correct. The impacts are likely to occur somewhere along a line from southeastern California near Yuma, Arizona to northern Lea County in eastern New Mexico. I can't be any more specific than that. Sorry."

"What size...um...what sort of damage will they

do and would you recommend we move everyone inside on the chance they hit anywhere near here?"

"Wouldn't be a bad idea since we happen to be on that line," Sandra Klein said. "They are so dim that they are difficult to pick out from everything else up there...and that says they are large enough to make fine powder out of a small town."

"If you don't mind," Emery Klein began, "I'd like to be outside during the event."

"Emery Klein."

"What? Are you out of your mind?"

"No."

"Yes, he is. Don't pay any attention to him."

* * *

18 October 2059: 0830 MST

Dr. Norman Salzman was on the other end of the connection. Emery Klein could plainly tell by his expression that he was strained and not the jovial character he had known in school during the "good old days." Back when they would swap lies about profs, fellow students...and conquests both knew never happened while draining a pitcher of ice cold ale in a small bar that was conveniently situated close to the student center.

"Hello, Norm. How goes the battle down there?"

"No better than anywhere else, I imagine. But we're not going to be able to stay here much longer, my friend. Have any room left up there?"

"Yeah. Plenty. Come on up when you're ready.

How many are working with you now?"

"It's down to four of us. Seems like everyone else had some place they just had to go. Are you ready for your update?"

"Yeah, let's have it."

"All the data we got I've already transmitted to your system, but the string you saw is made up of eleven individuals. The first two and the last one are going to miss us, but not by much. That's a good thing, too, because they're big guys, six hundred meters and more. Eight of them are going to make it to impact. One on the moon, the other seven here. The last one in the parade, one of those that is going to miss us, will be a grazer that will yield one stupendous light show.

"The first impactor is a small one and it's going to come down in the Pacific about five hundred and eighty klicks west and three degrees south of San Diego. That will occur on 12 December at twenty-three hours and eighteen minutes your time.

"Due to its minimal size it will probably generate a Tsunami of about eight meters, maybe a little higher, when it reaches shore in San Diego and along the Baja coast. The second is a shade bigger and will hit real close to Ensenada. Maybe 15 klicks east of the town. Nobody wants to be anywhere near there when it does because it's going to make a brand new bay and Ensenada will be at the bottom of it.

"Then we have the next three. Any one of them alone wouldn't do much damage, just fifty—maybe sixty meters of rock each—but they're acting like a single body and two of them are going to go off

201

over the middle of downtown Yuma. Not much in the way of a crater—sky burst...fairly high—but they'll do a lot of damage because of the air blast over-pressure and heat. The other one will kick up the dust about ten klicks east—but they're all going to explode at about the same time. That's another place you wouldn't want to be.

"Number six is roughly three hundred meters in its largest dimension and is going to hit forty-five plus klicks east of Alamogordo at the eastern edge of the pines, basically in the middle of nowhere. No real blast damage to Alamogordo, but it'll give them ten centimeters or more of ejecta and crap. It could cause some roofs to cave in and it's going to shake the hell out of them. About seven on the Richter. No doubt it'll set the woods on fire and leave a crater some seven and a half klicks across.

"Number seven is going to be of particular interest and concern to you.

The impact point will be about sixty plus klicks due east of your location. It's big enough—half a klick—to make it down to impact. I don't know what you did to deserve this, but I hope you guys built well because you're going to get a jolt close to eight on the scale and you don't want to be outside for this one, believe me. Do you think you can get us some visible light pics and a spectrographic shot of the fireball from the impact?"

"Of course we can. Have you—"

"I know what you're going to ask and the answer is, yes. We contacted all the areas that will be affected and we have been assured that evacuation of anyone still around in those places will take place well before the predicted impacts."

"Good. Thanks, Norm. So, when are you coming up here?"

"Duh! What do you think? After I hear you survived your close impactor, man."

* * *

20 November 2059: 1940 MST

News of the coming impacts spread fast through the population south of the border. Not fast enough north of the line. Tecate was filling with people from Tijuana to as far south as Veintesiete de Enero. With such a mass movement the Mexican troops were forced to go east to maintain some semblance of control over the situation. People north of the border, in and around San Ysidro and Otay Mesa, were quick to seize the opportunity and easily overpowered the few troops and aduanales remaining at the two far western border crossings. Eighty-four lives were lost in the ensuing gun battles. After the shooting died down, a flood of anglos poured across the line and began their slow movement south, most on foot, the rest on bycicles.

Of those who managed to cross into Mexico, few knew anything more than that they were heading south and fled for what appeared to them to be the most direct route—the coast highway—a path that would lead them directly to Ensenada. The majority of them had no experience with Mexico and didn't speak Spanish. They were already exhausted from their journey to San Ysidro on minimal food and inadequate water. Then the long wait before the line was breached. They marched off with their burdens of belongings—burdens that would bring them to grief if they couldn't get well south of Ensenada before the event. An event that was a scant fifty-three days away.

* * *

25 November 2059: 1030 MST

The sun, plump and hazy orange, rose seemingly against its will over the Permian basin and was promptly swallowed into a pool of thick, low lying clouds. The unseasonable heat had retreated and had been replaced by a biting cold that attacked the lungs and nipped at nasal passages not given the opportunity to adjust.

Daniel Klein clapped gloved hands together and danced in a tight circle while Wendell Stone worked the combination into the outer door's locking mechanism.

"Will you hurry up with that?" he said through clattering teeth.

"Big, tough Traveler like you can't take a little drop in the temp? How are you going to handle it when it really gets cold?"

"This is not 'a little drop in the temp' and it's not going to be that cold on my watch, man. I'll leave that problem to those who come later. If you don't mind, that is."

"I wouldn't make any bets on how fast it's going to get really cold if I were you, Dan. Your brother told me that when the conditions are right it'll be a matter of weeks before we're—ah, got it—in the deep freeze. After you, sir."

The massive outer door rolled open on the first entry chamber and Daniel Klein jumped inside, out of the wind that was building on top of the bluff. Stone slipped in behind him and tons of concrete and steel outer door closed with a solid thud that moved the pad beneath their feet. Banks of LEDs overhead gave off a cool blue-white glow and cast complex shadow patterns to the floor.

"Still doing interviews?"

"Yeah, but this is the last few, unless we get some stragglers later on.

Then we can close this place up until we're sure there aren't more little pieces coming down in our territory."

"Sure? How can you be sure...if you can't see the damned things until they're ready to land on us?"

"Saw these in time, didn't we?"

"Luck of the draw, man. You just happened to be looking in the right place at the right time. Like your kid says, 'It's a big, big sky out there.' Damn. Sure."

"Okay, I can't argue with that. But we're connected with several observatories still reporting and that cuts the odds by a chunk and a half."

"What kind of BS, forked tongue, double-talking crap is that? A chunk and a half."

* * *

Stoker moved the M-191 as close to the northwestern facing wall of the ravine as he could get it, shut it down and sealed it. He checked again to make sure none of the boulders were large enough to do any damage if they were knocked loose and tumbled down on the APC. Satisfied, he made his way to the entrance of the bunker where several engineers were preparing to close the outer doors.

All of the men at the entrance jerked to attention and saluted smartly when he approached.

"Begging the General's pardon, sir, but are these things that are coming down on Yuma very big?" a youthful lieutenant asked.

"No, son. There's nothing much to worry about where we are. They'll be detonating a long way from here, and they're all quite small. What we're doing is merely precautionary, Lieutenant. We're can't be absolutely certain about the actual detonation point. We were informed they'd go off over Yuma but, if they explode over our location, we don't want to be outside, do we?"

"Yes, sir. I mean, no, sir. Thank you, sir."

The young lieutenant appeared to be genuinely relieved. After all, those calming, reassuring words came from a general and generals are supposed to know things, Stoker thought, grinning inwardly. Something needs to be done about the stiffness around here, though. Something that won't break down discipline and respect for authority. What?

Stoker returned the barely twenty-five year old

marine's salute and went inside.

***

25 November 2059: 1035 PST

"Oh, man. Look at all the hotels, Janette. I'll bet they're all empty, too. Looks like the people who lived here already went south."

"Yeah, it does. I noticed all the businesses on the way in were closed, too. I've...I've always wanted a vacation in Mexico. Do you think we could stay here for a few days before we move on? Just to rest up? Please, Michael, please."

"Sure, sweetheart. What's a couple of weeks of luxury going to hurt? There's probably lots of food and stuff in the stores we could grab, too. Besides, we won't have another chance like this for a long time and, to tell you the truth, I'm just flat beat. You tell the kids we're going over to...um...the El Conquistador while I get our stuff inside. We have to hurry, though. It looks like a lot of other people have the same idea and we don't have a reservation."

Seventeen days to impact.

***

25 November 2059: 1400 MST

Carolyn Drake padded down the spongy gray carpet to Mel's apartment in Whites City. She tapped softly on the door, then stuck her head in.

207

The aroma of dead cigarettes and stale boiled coffee greeted her.

"Um...have you seen Dyllan?"

"Uh, yeah. I saw him a couple of hours ago with that Stahl guy. They went up to the caverns to talk to Wendell about the final installation of the big generators in the main buildings," Mel said. "Say, I'm working on the set-up for the Caveman Chronicle. Want to keep yourself busy while we wait for our call?"

"Thanks, but I don't have the time right now. I'm helping Lolly and the others with the big dinner for tonight. I never realized what an incredible job it was to make a dinner for so many people. But keep me in mind for the future, okay? I've always wanted to be a writer, just scared to death of doing anything about it."

"Well, since you know the whole staff, it's a shoo-in," Mel said and laughed out loud. "And I really could use the help, if you're interested."

* * *

25 November 2059: 1700 MST

"Okay, now, what's the news, Norm? All good, I hope." Emery Klein said and adjusted the hue brightness control upward to naturalize the color. I'll have to tell Dyllan about that before it dies and everyone turns uniformly green, or something worse, he thought.

"Not all good, I'm afraid. The one that's going to hit in the Pacific west of San Diego is bigger than we had originally estimated. The Tsunami generated from that one will top twelve meters—more like fifteen. And the one that's going to hit Ensenada is larger, too. The projected size of the crater from that one will be more like sixteen kilometers. It's okay, though.

The Mexican authorities told us the whole region has been totally evacuated. All the rest remain the same. How's it going up there?"

"We're making final preparations to close up for this impact.

Everything appears to be going according to plan and we're having a grand banquet up here tonight to celebrate being locked in like so many nuts in a rocky asylum. Too bad you can't be here."

"We'll open an extra can of stew to compensate. Have you found anything else on your sweeps?"

"No, but, if we do, you'll be the first to hear about it. Eyes to the sky, Norm."

* * *

27 November 2059: 1200 PST

"You know what day this is, Michael?"

"Sure. It's the twenty-seventh of November. I haven't forgotten our anniversary again, have I?"

"No, dingwit. Our anniversary is on the twelfth of December. This is Thanksgiving Day. It's Thanksgiving and we don't have a turkey for the first time in twenty-four years."

"S'pose we can make this chile taste like

209

turkey?"

"No—we can't make that chile taste like turkey. You're crazy. You know that? Certifiably nuts. Wanna go down to the beach?"

"Now look who's crazy. The kids are down there and they'll just throw sand at us again."

"Can we...um...stay here until after Christmas?"

"Sure. Why not? We still have electricity—last time I checked, anyway. The food's great, except for no turkey. We have all the bottled gas the barbecue can use. We have an endless supply of clean sheets and stuff. The stores are open whenever we want something and their freezers are freezing things like they should. We have a great view, and the hotel rates would be hard to beat anywhere. On top of all that, it's not too crowded and we've made some nice friends here. Several of them are planning on doing the same thing. Did you know that?"

"No. Really?"

"Yeah. I was talking to Warren McCall this morning, and his family's staying...all fifteen of them—gakh! He said that several of the families he knows are going to wait until New Year's Day before they leave. Sort of fitting, don't you think? A brand new experience for a brand new year."

"Okay. New Year's Day, then?"

"Deal."

Fifteen days to impact.

* * *

1 December 2059: 0930 MST

210

Jeremy let himself into the office without knocking. He was more than a little upset with the Kleins for running him out of the observatory when he wanted to tinker with the mount drives to take some of the positioning errors out of them. His father was sitting, bent over one of the monitors on his desk. He didn't look happy at all.

"Why the sour face, dad?"

"Oh, hi, Jeremy. I didn't hear you come in. How's the observatory coming along?"

"Good, I guess...when the crummy Kleins let me have a shot at it, anyway. I know, dad. They have lots of stuff they need to do and it's really important and all...but I'd sure like to have more time on it. Anyway, how come you look so worried?"

"I don't know. I think maybe because I'm concerned about what's going to happen when we're all locked inside. You know. How everybody's going to get along when they're faced with the reality of it all."

"What was it you told me about going to the university and living in the dorms?"

"You're right. Let things happen as they will and make the best of it.

Don't let the boobs ruin your day, right? Where have you been, man? I haven't seen much of you at all for the last four or five months."

"Not my fault, dad. You're the one who has been too busy with everything to notice. Mom said the same thing."

"She did? It's...true, I guess."

211

"You know it's true."

"Yeah. You're right. Time to change all that. Hey, how about we go down to the city for lunch? I'll bet we can talk your mom into making some extra-thick, juicy Braunschweiger sandwiches with all the trimmings. Sound good?"

"Yeah...but it's only nine-thirty."

"Is it? Okay. Brunch, then."

***

6 December 2059: 1200 PST

"Janette. Feast your eyes on what I found."

"Where...where did you get that?"

"In the walk-in freezer of that big store at the north end of town. It looks like no one has the energy to go that far—the freezer's full of things."

"Fantastic. Turkey for Christmas dinner. Is our freezer big enough for it?"

"Oh yeah. I couldn't find any cranberry sauce, but I did find a lot of stuffing mix and instant mashed potatoes."

"Great. We'll be able to celebrate, after all. All the kids at the table and—"

"You're not going to invite anyone else, right?"

"Oh, Michael."

Six days to impact.

***

8 December 2059: 1530 MST

212

Robin Stahl peered into the security screen for the surveillance camera at the top entrance where a young couple stood, pushing at the buttons on the outer pad. Beyond them in the parking lot sat a tractor-trailer rig. He keyed the intercom.

"Wendell, we have a youngish couple at the outer door poking at the pad. No sign of any others and there's an eighteen-wheeler in the lot. Shall I let'em in?"

"Yeah. We still have plenty of room, but be sure it's only the two of them. Anyone else will have to wait a couple of hours. Send them straight in to me and I'll process them now."

"You got it."

* * *

Stone couldn't miss how the man's gaze kept moving from full eye contact down to his nameplate on the desk, then back to his face. Nervous? Worried about something more than being vaporized by a falling rock? He couldn't say, but something about the man's reactions caused him to make a note to watch the two of them for a while.

"All right. Here are the keys to your apartment. It's on the second tier down, but I'm afraid it's on the fourth floor. Just ask anyone up there and they'll be able to direct you to it."

"Yes, sir. Thank you."

"Make sure you read through our policies and regulations for governing this community. They will be strictly enforced. Do you understand?"

They both nodded in the affirmative.

213

"There will be an orientation session for our late arrivals in the main meeting room on the lower level tomorrow at oh-eight-thirty. Make sure you're there. Um...one more thing and we're all set. The spelling on that name—was it one "L" or two?"

"S-c-o-one el-i-n-i."

* * *

12 December 2059: 2325 PST

It was a dark night. They could see the bobbing beams from the children's flashlights as than ran and skipped along the beach. Michael took Janette's hand in his and played the light over the waves on the shore.

"Oh, Michael. Thank you so much for a special day. I even loved the card, even though I couldn't read it."

"I couldn't either, but it had something on it that looked like 'anniversary,' so I grabbed it. Pretty card, though, wasn't it?"

The utter darkness was overtaken by a dim but brightening light.

Bright enough to make shadows and light up the breakers. Michael looked up and gasped. "What is that, Michael?"

"A super-nova, I think. Our twenty-fifth anniversary and even the heavens are here to celebrate with us. I saw a show on those once. There was one so bright that it could be seen during daylight. And the ancient Chinese reported one bright enough to cast shadows...like this one. I don't

214

remember when they said that happened, but it had to be a long time ago or they wouldn't have said 'ancient Chinese,' would they?"

"Oh, wow. It's getting brighter, Michael. I'm so happy right now, I could—"

Impact.

To be Continued